D1564004

Half Moon Pocosin

Half Moon Pocosin

Cherry L.F. Johnson

Academy Chicago Publishers

Published by
Academy Chicago Publishers
Chicago, Illinois 60610

Library of Congress Cataloging-in-Publication Data

Johnson, Cherry Lurae Flake.
Half Moon Pocosin / Cherry Lurae Flake Johnson.
p. cm.
ISBN 0-89733-438-8 (hc)
I. Title.
PS3560.03736H34 1997
813'.54—dc20 96-25532
CIP

Half Moon Pocosin is dedicated to my parents,
Charles and Lurae, and my husband Wayne.
Thank you for your love and support.

I would like to thank Karla Holloway, Angela Davis Gardner and Lee Smith for their advice, support, and concern.

Also, I wish to thank John Kessel and David Covington for their advice on earlier drafts of my manuscript.

○ Contents ○

1	Cindy	9
2	In the Fields	23
3	A Shadow	35
4	A Song	45
5	Sam	67
6	The Rain	79
7	Ghosts	111
8	The Visit	137
9	At the Fair	151
10	The Women	161

1

○ Cindy ○

Eastern North Carolina
Summer, 1933

J.D. rolled over when Cindy got out of bed, but he was asleep again before she got to the bedroom door. She could always tell when he went back to sleep by the way he breathed, drawing in slow, deep breaths and letting them out in the same easy way. She closed the door behind her and went through the hall to the kitchen. J.D. had done a right good job on the hall when he closed it in the week before. She had told him how cold it was to walk through there of a morning in the dead of winter.

Cindy reached up and pulled the string hanging from the light. J.D. had finally agreed to get electricity from those new lines because he said he could see better at night to whittle. Blinking in the sudden brightness, she opened the stove door and put in the morning's first piece of wood.

When J.D. had brought in the wood the night before, she asked him if they might could get one of them new stoves like some of the folks had at town. J.D. could hook one up to work just like the lights since that company had run lines to the country. But he said they cost too much. Besides, if that stove had been good enough for his mama, why wasn't it good enough for Cindy? He was proud to do things just the way his father did them. J.D. chopped all the wood they used, stacking part of it between two trees in the back yard where the sap could dry out. He kept dried wood under the back porch. It stayed there till he or Cindy carried a few pieces at a time into the house.

She put the last stick of wood in the stove and left the door standing open. Then she tore a page from the Sears and Roebuck catalogue and laid the page in a chair on the back porch as she went outside.

Walking to the outhouse, Cindy felt the beads of dew collect between her toes and on top of her feet. Those same beads broke and trickled, tickling her feet as she walked back to the house. Lucky thing there weren't no close neighbors to see her walk outside in her flannel nightgown. The Partins were the nearest neighbors, but even they were not within sight. J.D. and Cindy's place stood alone in Half Moon Pocosin.

J.D.'s great-grandfather was the first man in the county brave enough to live in the 'cosin. J.D. liked to remind people of that when they said they wouldn't live in them haunted woods for nothing in this world. They couldn't stand the isolation—just the Spears' house and fields cut out of the woods that lined each side of the dirt road that curved 'round in an arc.

On the porch Cindy crumpled the catalogue page into a loose wad and wet one side with kerosene from the tin can in the corner. As she screwed the rusty cap back on the can, a silky breeze slipped across her shoulders. It was one of those strange half-warm, half-cool gusts of air that seemed to come from nowhere before the sun warmed things up on a summer morning. Cindy turned around expecting to see someone, but nobody was there.

She crammed the soggy paper between two pieces of kindling and lit the stove. While she was waiting for the stove to get hot, she went back into the bedroom without making a sound. It was about time for baby Callie to wake. Cindy wanted to get the baby before she cried and woke J.D.

Cindy lifted Callie from the wooden cradle beside her bed. J.D. had made it himself nights after he came in from working. He had set it right there by the side of the bed Cindy slept on so she could get to the baby real easy during the night.

She carried Callie to the kitchen, rubbing her cheek against the soft, fuzzy baby hair as she walked. It felt the way a chick or little duck does before the adult feathers start to grow. In the kitchen Cindy laid Callie on a pallet she made by folding a quilt into quarters on the floor. She looked at her baby. Callie was so perfect. Cindy wondered how such a tiny person could have all the parts that people do. The most amazing thing was how Callie could have such tiny fingernails and toenails.

"Stay right there, angel. Mama's got to cook," Cindy said.

After she laid strips of bacon in the pan, Cindy lifted Callie from the quilt. She liked to touch her baby. She steadied Callie on the edge of the counter with one hand and turned the bacon over in the pan for the first time with the other. With the bacon starting to fry good, Cindy went on with the business of diaper changing. Again, she went to the back porch, opened the lid of an empty lard stand and dropped in the dirty diaper. As she started back inside, the breeze stole the screen door from her fingertips and slammed it. The noise scared Callie, and she began to cry.

"Shhh," Cindy said.

But the baby kept on.

Cindy began to sing.

Sweet little Callie, don't you cry,
Or the bad ghost will get you by and by.
But if you're good and act real nice,
The good ghost will bring you sugar and spice.

Callie quieted, and Cindy was able to go on with her cooking. She put eggs on to boil and set a jar of pear preserves on the table. She saw Callie wrinkling her face again. "Callie, Callie, please don't cry."

J.D. walked into the kitchen. "Ain't no need for you to keep singing that song, Cindy. I done told you you're gonna scare that child. Or else you'll have her singing that foolish stuff soon as she can talk."

"It's just a song."

"Well, sing something else."

She put Callie down and turned the bacon over in the pan. The grease splattered, burning the back of her hand like it had so many times before. She mumbled under her breath and touched her lips to the small pink spot the grease had left. Was it the bacon that sent grease flying, or was it the pan? Maybe it was just her pan. She remembered the day her mama gave her that black iron frying pan. It was the day she got married.

"You better take this," Mama said. "You'll be needing it. A hard-working boy like J.D. has got to eat."

And Mama was right. There wasn't a day that came that she didn't use that pan.

Callie began to fuss. Sitting on the kitchen floor wasn't half as nice as sitting on the edge of her mother's hip, tucked into the curve of her waist.

Cindy picked her up and held her with one arm.

"You hold that baby too much," J.D. said. His dark, uncombed hair stood straight up.

He was standing at the back door looking out toward the garden. Cindy wondered what he was thinking about—how much rain it would take for a good crop, probably.

"Your breakfast is ready," she said.

He looked sort of like a scarecrow in the morning. What's the use of fixing up hair, he always said, just to go to the field? And with his patched work clothes—well, he was a sight.

She mashed up an egg in a saucer with her fork for Callie to eat. She hummed while she worked and almost started singing, but caught herself in time.

J.D. ate his breakfast without saying a word.

Cindy fed Callie her egg and gave her some of the sweet syrupy juice from the jar of preserves.

"I'll be out in the field the other side of the barn," J.D. said as he went out the door.

She gave Callie some milk and sat down to eat her own breakfast. Cindy barely chewed before she swallowed. The beans were ready, and she wanted to pick them before it got real hot.

After breakfast, she spread a blanket under the big gum tree at the east end of the garden. That would keep the sun off Callie. No telling just how old that tree was. J.D. said his grandpa told him it was there when he was a boy, far back as he could remember. And the roots went out so far that you couldn't start your garden rows for a good twenty feet from the tree. Cindy put the baby on the blanket and went into the garden with her bucket.

She picked for more than an hour, long enough to get three-fourths of the beans, glancing occasionally to be sure the baby hadn't crawled off her blanket.

Cindy felt an emptiness inside. It was the same sinking feeling she had in her stomach last summer when Ray Darden's crop was ruined. She had told J.D. that something bad was going to happen, but he said it was just because she was expecting. But sure enough, J.D. heard the next week at town how the hail had beaten down Ray's crop.

She stood straight up and stiffened as the wind slithered through the leaves. Branches made cracking sounds, and the leaves turned their slightly silver undersides up the way they do right before a storm. She looked across the field at the stand of trees down by the creek. They didn't seem to be moving at all. And there wasn't a cloud in the sky.

She picked up her bucket, headed for the tree and grabbed Callie and the blanket up into one arm. With the blanket dragging over the still-damp ground, she went into the house.

While Callie napped, Cindy snapped her beans into inch-long sections and washed them. Then she put them in a pot to boil with a chunk of ham.

By the time the baby woke up and J.D. came in around noon, she had finished cooking the beans, made a pan of biscuits, and cleaned the kitchen.

"I saw where you stopped picking," J.D. said as they sat down to eat. "Why didn't you finish that piece of row?"

"I'll get 'em tomorrow," she said.

"That ain't what I asked you. What you been doing all morning?"

Cindy rubbed her hand along the rough underside of the table. It was rectangular, made of plain wood that splintered easily on the bottom and legs where it had not been sanded.

"Picking beans and keeping house," she said. "Besides, the wind got to blowing."

"Cindy, you beat all I've ever seen," he said. His hair stood higher than ever, and his blue eyes became a colder gray. "There I am out there working in them fields all day, and you're up here scared of every little thing you hear. Now it's the wind. That's just the way all your folks are, all the time believing in stuff that just ain't there."

"Ain't nothing wrong with my folks," she said quietly.

"Ain't nothing right with them either," he said.

They finished their meal in silence.

When he left the table, J.D. went to the bedroom and took off his shirt. The afternoon would be a scorcher, he said, so he wore no shirt under his overalls.

"I'll be farther out this time," he told her as he left for the field.

Cindy washed the dishes in her enamel-coated dishpan. Then she went outside to feed the chickens. J.D. usually milked the cow because she liked to kick sometimes, but the chickens were left to Cindy's care.

She sprinkled ground corn from the bucket. The hens came running and gathered 'round her feet, pecking at the corn as if she hadn't fed them the day before. "Silly chicks," she said. "You act more like pigs."

She made her rounds in the fenced-in chicken yard, gathering the eggs, putting them in the bucket she'd just emptied. As she moved from nest to nest, wood boxes filled with straw, she carried Callie pressed into her side by her free arm.

One hen that she called "Old Flossie" was determined to set on her nest. When Cindy stuck her hand into the clump of straw, the chicken squawked, fluttered, and jumped from the nest, quickly strutting over to where the other chickens were still pecking at the corn J.D. had raised and had ground at the mill for them. Cindy ignored the hen, but Callie began to cry.

"Oh, Flossie, look what you've done."

Callie wailed louder.

Cindy looked toward the back of the house. The boards had been whitewashed, but the coating was peeling, leaving bare wood exposed to the weather. She began pacing back and forth, three steps toward the house, turn, four or five steps toward the hog pen built so that one side of it was an outer wall of the barn, turn, all the while never leaving the mesh-wire chicken yard. Still Callie wouldn't hush.

"*Callie, Callie, no need to cry . . .*"

Cindy sang until Callie was quiet. By this time, she had gotten all the eggs and gone inside.

Cindy put Callie to bed for her afternoon nap, and went out on the back porch to wash clothes.

She remembered another thing her mama had said; a woman's washing is never done.

Like always, Mama was right.

Sweat poured down her neck and back in little rivers that ended at the soaked waistband of her skirt, and her fingers turned bright pink as she rubbed the clothes back and forth on the washboard. She scrubbed the clothes carefully. If you didn't rub long enough, everything would still be dirty. Rub too long or too hard, and you'd wear a hole right through the material.

She worked on the stains on the knees of the overalls J.D. had worn the day before. The knees of his breeches were always the first place to go. Every pair he had except those he wore to church had patches on the fronts of the legs. What else could she do? J.D. got on his knees when he milked the cow instead of sitting on the three-legged stool his mama had always used. He crawled on all fours under the house to get out wood. Cindy wondered why he didn't squat and reach under like she did. It really didn't matter. What mattered was that J.D. always had dirt ground into the knees of his pants. She cleaned them as gently as she could, but she had to get them clean. She washed them till holes appeared as if mice had chewed on the pants legs. Then she patched them.

Cindy dumped the water in the galvanized washtub. She always washed the dirtiest clothes last, and today, like most days, the overalls were last. She pumped a little more water into the bottom of the foot tub, swished it around, and dumped it again to get the grit out of the bottom. Then she stood at the clothesline, pulling wrung-out clothes from the tub and pinning them up one piece at a time.

Slowly a chill enveloped her body, sending signals that carried her back to another time of the year. She felt as cold as she had last winter at hog-killing time. She and J.D. had shivered as they worked outside to safeguard the slaughtered hogs from spoiling before the meat was put in the smokehouse to cure.

But it wasn't winter now. She pinned the last shirt on the line and went inside. She felt instantly warmer. No chill in the air in there, only the heat from the stove.

She peeled the potatoes she had gotten from the basket under the house. Mama had always told her potatoes would keep longer in a cool, dark place.

She had to stop to get Callie, but she put her on the floor to play with her little stuffed dolly Cindy's mama had made from old clothes. Callie played while Cindy finished peeling, humming a lullaby as she worked. Then she put the potatoes on to boil, took a book from under her Sunday apron in a drawer and sat down at the table. Callie made soft, happy noises as she beat the small ragdoll against her own leg. Cindy opened the book Miss Elbert had brought to her and started reading where she had stopped the day before. It took a long time to read even one book. It was hard to find time to read.

Cindy knew when the potatoes started to boil without getting up. She could hear the water bubbling, some of it splashing out onto the stove.

J.D. came in just as Cindy was closing the book.

"Supper ready?" he asked.

"Not yet, but it won't be long. Ain't you back early?"

J.D. stood there looking at her, started to walk away, and then turned back toward her again.

"Wasn't that you out there by the barn calling me to come in?"

"No," she said.

J.D. drew his eyebrows closer together and scratched the back of his head.

"You sure?" he asked.

"I didn't call you."

He sat in a chair at the table and stared out the back door. Cindy watched him.

"J.D.?"

"What?"

"I've told you strange things happen 'round here."

"There you go again. Once you get something in that head of yours, you just keep on and on."

Cindy carried the pot of potatoes out to the back porch and poured the water onto the ground below, taking care not to lose any of the potatoes.

"I reckon it's them books you read that puts mess like that in your head. I done told you to tell that school teacher to quit bringing them to you. Don't she know you got something to do 'sides read all day?"

"I don't read all day," she said. "Just every now and again when I got a minute."

"Don't tell me. I seen you hiding that book when I was coming in a while ago."

J.D. pulled open the drawer where Cindy had put the book. He pulled it out, letting her good apron fall to the floor.

"Moll Flanders," he read. "I bet it's 'bout a ghost or something. That's all you like is something that don't make no sense."

"No. It's good. It's about this woman—"

"Well, ain't that something? A woman that ain't got enough to do so she reads about another woman."

Cindy let her head droop, her neck unable to support its burden. She turned away so he wouldn't see her crying.

"Women," he muttered to himself.

That night she lay in bed listening to the crickets. Beside her, J.D. breathed with his same sleeping rhythm. She wondered why she ever told him anything at all.

2

○ In the Fields ○

Cindy rolled the pieces of biscuit dough between her hands, making each one the same size as the one before it. She didn't have to measure or even look to compare the biscuits. She felt it. After you made them every day, twice or three times a day for so long, you just felt it. Always the same shape. Always the same size and weight.

The first thing she could remember was her mama making biscuits. Mama's hands were about the color of sourwood honey, browned a little from the sun, but speckled with flour. Her palms were white, but not as white as the speckles. Mama called them her biscuit bugs when Cindy asked what they were—"little drops of splattered milk that dried up under the flour," she said.

When Cindy was a young child, her mama used to sit her on the work table while she was making up a pan of biscuits or rolling out her pastries and pies. "Might as well get used to the kitchen now," Mama said sometimes. Cindy hadn't understood then.

Cindy cooked breakfast earlier these days. Now that the crop was starting to come in, J.D. had to be in the field sooner. Cindy helped him all she could, but she still had to cook and keep the house. If they only had more money, they could hire some hands for the whole summer. But J.D.said they could only hire help at the very busiest time. There just wasn't enough money to keep somebody all summer and down into the fall. J.D. would have to pay a hand right much, and Cindy would have to cook enough dinner to feed him, too.

But soon they would have to get a hand, at least for a little while. That was a fact of life in those parts. Farmers either kept hired hands or had children that could help. Papa and Mama didn't hire help. They hadn't for years. But they had Jasper and Joe Ray to help. Cindy could remember when they were younguns how Papa would stand Joe Ray and Jasper under the shelter to hand tobacco. He said the two of them handing ought to be equal to a grown hand passing the leaves along to the next person. She had helped sometimes, too. Papa used to stand her up on top of a cinder block so she would be tall enough to do the work.

Cindy's brothers still worked for Papa, and now her little sister Kelly was standing on the block to hand tobacco, but Cindy's place was here. She had to help J.D. and be a good mama to Callie.

Sometimes it all seemed to happen so fast, and she wondered how she got here on J.D.'s farm from Papa's. Sometimes she would wake up in the morning and breathe that first conscious breath and smell the tilled dirt, and in that gray second, between sleep and waking, she would think she was in her little bed at Mama and Papa's house and that Kelly was in the same room near her on the other small bed.

Then she would hear J.D. breathing beside her, not yet awake. She would open her eyes and see Callie asleep in the cradle by the bed and sometimes be surprised at first that she was her baby—hers, not Mama's or anybody else's, but hers—and that she had to get going and cook for J.D. and take care of her baby. But even on those mornings when Cindy's life seemed separated from her, she knew what she had to do. And she would go into the kitchen and fix breakfast just like she was doing right now.

She put the pan of biscuits into the oven. Biscuits and molasses was what kept a poor family going, Mama had said. Most folks in the county were poor. Cindy wondered what it would be like to not have to worry so much about money.

Papa told her she'd better count her blessings. He and Mama had always scraped up enough for her to eat, and now she had J.D. At least he had land and could farm and could feed her, Papa had said. That was something to be thankful for in 1933.

That was how she got here, she supposed. Because Papa thought he was doing what was right for her. Papa said that any man that couldn't feed his wife and younguns till they were big enough to do it theirselves wasn't much of a man at all. A man had to be careful, too, Papa said, about who he let marry his girls. It was up to a girl's pa to see to it that the boy she was marrying could take care of her. Only decent for a man to look after his gal like that.

Papa had tried hard to do the right thing. She knew he had. But he just didn't understand. He didn't understand at all that she wanted something different.

And it wasn't just Papa that didn't understand. Nobody understood but Miss Elbert.

Miss Elbert was Cindy's best friend, if you could call her that. She really couldn't say she had what you really might call friends like she did when she was a schoolgirl.

She didn't have the time to go off visiting. And if she did, J.D. wouldn't like it none. He didn't like it much when Miss Elbert came out to the farm to see her, but at least he hadn't said anything to Cindy's used-to-be school teacher to keep her from coming to visit.

Janie, as Cindy now called her, came out every couple of weeks or so. Just out of the blue, she would come and bring another book. Cindy would hear a wagon coming and go to the door and look, and there she'd be coming up in the yard. She'd be right dusty if it hadn't rained in a while, and some of the red hair she had carefully pinned up that morning would be loose, falling around her face. Even so, she was quite pretty, Cindy thought.

J.D. didn't think she was pretty at all. Not many folks 'round there did. They called her a foreigner, even though her family had been in America just as long as their families had. J.D. said that was where that burnt-looking hair came from—foreigners. He said all them freckles and them cat eyes didn't help none neither. Cindy had long since given up on trying to tell him that Janie was pretty just because of that, because she was different. Anybody could have the same brown hair and plain skin. Some folks said that was how come she was teaching school and wasn't married, because she wasn't much of nothing to look at. But they almost always added that she wasn't getting paid to look pretty, and she was a right good teacher.

Now Cindy, she was pretty, they said. Folks had always told her`Mama and Papa she was. That was how come she could've had her pick of two men, her grandmother said. Most girls had to do a lot of smiling and sweet talking to land one, but Cindy didn't have to do a thing and had two looking at her, Granda said.

But Cindy didn't feel pretty. She felt tired and most of the time she wasn't sure where she belonged.

She took the biscuits out of the oven and set them on the table.

In the bedroom she nudged J.D.'s arm. He turned his head and mumbled, but he went back to sleep. She pushed his arm harder.

"J.D., get up. Biscuits are gonna get cold."

She went 'round the bed to the cradle and picked up Callie.

"Get up now."

Cindy carried the baby to the kitchen, leaving J.D. alone to dress.

After he had gone to the field, she picked tomatoes from the garden and washed them at the pump on the back porch. She could slice them at dinner, and they would have tomato sandwiches and the corn she had left over from supper the night before. She didn't have time to cook big dinners when she worked in the field.

Cindy was in the field pulling lugs from the ripening tobacco less than an hour after J.D. had started. She didn't like priming those bottom leaves. She had to stoop way over, and by dinner time her back ached. J.D. said it was because she was a woman and was weak and that it didn't bother him none to bend over all day long. But she knew better. She had been at the end of the field and looked down a row and seen him stand up slow, not quite straight, with one arm raised to wipe sweat, the other behind him rubbing the small of his back. After dinner when they barned the tobacco, she knew he would not say that his shoulders got tired or that he was weak from the heat under the tin shelter.

Papa and her brothers were the same way, never letting on how hard the work was on their bodies. That was just the way men were, she guessed. Papa always said a man that wouldn't work when there wasn't nothing wrong with him was lazy, no account, not worth his salt. Said he was going to work out, not rust out. A little hard work never hurt nobody.

But Cindy knew it could. You had to work to eat or else you died, but if you worked hard you could die. Her grandpa died. Granda had found him in the field when she went to carry him some dinner. Couldn't talk plain, she said. Couldn't move one whole side of himself. A man who never had took a liking to no doctors laying in the dirt trying to ask for one. Pitiful, Granda had said. Pitiful. She had gone to town and gotten Dr Hedlin, but there wasn't much he could do. He said Grandpa had a stroke. Said if he had lived he wouldn't be able to walk or talk right. Might not even have had his right mind. He might be a baby in a grown man's body.

Cindy wished she could remember what her Grandpa had been like. She thought she could remember a big man holding her and the faint, sweet smell of cured tobacco. That must have been Grandpa. She hoped so. She hated to think that she might not remember him at all. Jasper could remember him real good, and Joe Ray could remember him fair. She felt cheated. They had been old enough when he died to remember how he used to play with them, and Kelly had never known him at all. But she was the one that had the sliver of a memory, that flash she called a recollection, that left her longing for more and ashamed that she could not call back much of a picture of a person she must have loved.

When she had primed all the tobacco she could hold in her arms, she went to the end of the row and laid it on the tobacco truck, a flat wooden cart with rusty rims 'round the wheels that the mule would pull to the shelter when it was full.

She went to check on Callie while she was out of the row. J.D. had made her a pen where she could sleep or play but not get herself hurt. That was the only way that Cindy could be free to help him. She didn't have nobody to watch the baby while she worked. He'd have to make her a bed soon, too, Cindy thought as she looked down at Callie, or else she'd have to sleep in the bed with them. Even though J.D. had made her cradle plenty big, there was only so long a baby could stay in it. She was getting too big, and Cindy was scared she'd wake up some morning, pull herself up, and fall out on her head. Ella Carson's boy had fallen on his head when he was a baby and didn't have the first lick of sense to this day. Mama said that was how come.

"Don't just stand there looking at that baby like she's gonna grow a foot 'fore dinner," J.D. said. He was putting tobacco on the truck.

"I was just checking her while I was this way," Cindy said.

"Well, I got 'bacca that's gonna burn up in the field if we don't get a move on. Need to have the lugs off half this field 'fore dinner."

She went back down the row to where she had stopped, priming and toting, priming and toting, till it was time to go to the house for dinner.

She went on to the house ahead of J.D. so she could fix their dinner right quick before he got there. She heated the corn and set two glasses of cool water on the table. She sliced the tomatoes at the counter and salted and peppered the slices before putting them between bread. She remembered how she had fixed tomato sandwiches back when she first met Sam, that traveling shoe salesman that came through town once a year. That was his favorite kind of sandwich, he had told her. She wondered now if it really had been or if he had just said that because he had heard her and Mama talking to Mr Parrish in the store at town when Mama was telling how they had the nicest tomatoes they'd had in five years. She remembered how mad Papa had been with her when he found out that she and Sam Barker had set in his car outside the schoolhouse one day at dinner and eaten those tomato sandwiches. Said he never thought he'd see the day when a gal of his did any such thing as that. And with a traveling salesman at that.

Cindy wondered where Sam was these days. She had heard that he'd been through town, but she hadn't seen him since then, and that was a good three months before she and J.D. got married. She wondered, like she had so many times, what it would be like to hardly ever stay at home, to go from town to town the way Sam did, talking to all sorts of people and seeing everything under the sun. She thought she might have liked it if she could have gone. She thought it must be something like reading a book, only you said and saw and smelled instead of reading it on the page and making a picture of the words in your head. Sam had been in seven states.He said he could take her to all of them. She'd never been out of the county more than two or three times, and then it was just across the line into the next county. Might as well say she'd never left home.

Might as well say she never would. She'd more than likely live out all her days here, slicing tomatoes, tending to younguns, bringing in the crop. Still, she couldn't help wondering some days what another life might be like, what having one of them motor cars and somebody to do your washing for you might be like.

But she was here, making tomato sandwiches, and Papa had thought that was what was best for her.

3

○ A Shadow ○

Cindy pulled the ears of corn from their stalks. This was the last corn of the year. She and J.D. had staggered planting the corn so that it would come off at four different times. That way, they'd have fresh corn the whole summer, and Cindy could keep up with getting it canned. She had already canned corn three times. No way she could put up enough corn for the whole fall and winter at one time.The corn would sour on the back porch, or the worms would get it in the garden.

She dragged the bushel baskets of corn one by one, tugging at the thin wire handles till she reached the ground just below the back porch where she would shuck and silk the corn. She sat down on the steps to rest. She had pulled corn all morning, and she still wouldn't be through if J.D. and Baxter hadn't helped her pull for an hour before they went to the field.

J.D. had hired Baxter right before the last batch of corn had come off. Baxter said he never knew it was so much work to pull corn. All he knew was that he had helped pull it when he was a boy. His mama and sisters had done the rest, except for getting up the shucks. His daddy used to make him get up all the shucks with the pitchfork and throw them to the cow and the mules.

Baxter was right good at telling when the corn was ready, though. Cindy always had to peel back the shucks a little on a couple of ears to be sure, but Baxter could just look at the ears, shucks and all, and tell you pretty near every time whether the corn was ready. He'd just always been able to do it, he said.

Cindy felt right sorry for him. There he was, helping other folks out wherever he could get work, when he wasn't raised that way. His daddy had raised him to think that a man was supposed to have his own land and tend it for himself.

But times were getting too hard. The bank had gotten Mr Bailey's farm a year and a half ago, and all he could do was let Baxter go out for hire and get his girls married off as soon as he could. Baxter's mama and daddy even had to move out of their house because the house was on their farm. Mr Bailey got a job clerking at the hardware store over in Graham, so they had moved to town. Their three girls were scattered 'round Beulah County, and Baxter was two counties away from where he ought to be.

Papa said that's the way things were going. Times were hard, mighty hard. Nowadays, if a man got his shirt tail just a little too long, got in just a little too much debt, he could go under before he knew what had happened. Papa said he didn't know what things were coming to.

Cindy reached down and picked up an ear of corn from the basket nearest to her. She peeled back the shucks about halfway. Perfect. Just like Baxter said it would be. Cindy held the corn in four curved fingers, sliding her thumb up and down the kernels.

Papa had always checked the corn himself before he'd let anybody pull the first ear. He'd always said there wasn't a bit of sense in pulling corn when it was too young. It just wasn't good, and there wasn't as much to eat either. Always best to be sure before you pulled it.

Cindy laid the corn back on top of the heap in the basket. Placing her palms flat on the step, she pushed herself up and went to the barn to get some sevin dust. She had seen a few holes in some of the collards when she was dragging the baskets from the garden.

She shook an old burlap bag of sevin over the tops of the collards. The poison covered the leaves with fine, white powder. She thought about how good the collards would be later on after the first frost had hit them. Why did the frost make a difference? Cindy never had known. She just knew that collards tasted better after the cold had got them. Her Mama would tell you so any day to the week.

In the barn she laid the toe sack back on top of the barrel where J.D. kept the sevin. Then she turned around and backed up against the barrel. Something was wrong. Suddenly there was a shadow on the floor in the door of the barn. It looked like a woman, the head toward Cindy, the wide long skirt fluttering as if it was being blown by the wind.

"J.D.? Baxter? Baxter, is that you? This ain't funny."

Cindy's voice trembled the same way her body did.

She kept looking at the shadow. It was right there, just inside the barn door. But nobody was there. Just a shadow with no one to make it. Nothing to stop the light from reaching inside the barn and to the floor. Cindy looked away, searching the barn with her eyes for the nearest tool or stick, but she could not reach anything without moving. She glanced back at the doorway, and the shadow was gone.

After long minutes, Cindy finally got the nerve up to go through the doorway and back to the house. Callie was crying in the bedroom. Cindy had left her napping an hour and a half ago while she finished pulling the corn, and the baby was wide awake now. Cindy fed Callie bread with peach jelly spread over it. She put fatback fried crisp in sliced biscuits for the men and herself. She boiled eggs, mashing their yolks up fine for deviled eggs. J.D. and Baxter would be in for dinner in a few minutes. She knew she had to get herself together before they came in, but she was still shaking a little. She couldn't make it stop. She didn't really want Baxter to see her all upset, and J.D. would get mad.

She heard J.D. and Baxter come up the steps and onto the back porch. She stepped sideways so that she could see them through the window. They were pumping water and washing up for dinner. When they came into the kitchen, she looked at them carefully. Neither one had on loose clothes that she thought might have been flapping in the wind if they had been near the barn. Cindy sat down at the table with them to eat.

"You gonna start shucking after dinner?" J.D. asked.

"Yeah," Cindy said. "Soon as y'all go back."

"How much you gonna shuck this evening, Cindy?" Baxter asked.

"Much as I can get blanched 'fore time to go to bed. I'll shuck more tomorrow."

"Why not just shuck it all and be done with it?"

"It'll dry out 'fore I could get it all put up."

"Oh."

"Y'all want some more?" Cindy asked them.

"Naw," J.D. said. "I'm full."

"How 'bout you, Baxter?"

"I b'lieve I'll have one more biscuit. They sure are good."

Cindy held the plate of biscuits out across the table to Baxter.

"I'll be ready soon as you finish eating," J.D. said. "I'll go 'head and get the stuff from the barn."

"I'll be right out," Baxter said.

J.D. went out the back door. Cindy stood up and looked out the window. She watched him till he went inside the barn.

"Baxter?"

"Huh?"

"Did one of y'all come up here to the barn this morning?"

"Naw. We didn't come back till dinner time."

"All right," Cindy said.

"Why, you think we ain't been working?" Baxter said, laughing.

"Just asking," she said, laughing a little too. "Thought I saw somebody is all."

"Wasn't us."

After J.D. and Baxter had gone back to the field, Cindy cut the pointed ends off the ears of corn and threw them into the pile. Then she peeled the shucks away from the corn, taking as many of the silks as she could away with the shucks, throwing them into the same pile. Callie crawled around inside the pen J.D. had brought up from the field. He would carry it back again when Cindy finished the corn and went back to help with bringing in the rest of the crop.

As the pile of shucks got bigger, she wondered if J.D. really knew how much work it was to put up corn. All he ever had to do was haul the shucks off and maybe pull a few bushels for her if she was lucky. He sat at the table and ate corn like it just appeared in the pot. At least Baxter did tell her "thank you" and "it was good" once in a while since he'd come there. She supposed J.D. thought the corn just appeared in the pot just like he thought his clothes appeared clean and folded in the chest in the bedroom.

Cindy remembered her mama putting up corn, summer after summer. Mama would always set a cane-bottomed chair out under a tree where it was cooler than in the kitchen. She'd shuck and silk till it was almost dark. Then she'd blanch and process jars long into the night.

Cindy thought about the first time she could remember her mama putting up corn. Mama was shucking the corn out under a tree, and Granda had come over to help her. Papa had made Jasper and Joe Ray stay 'round the house to throw the shucks to the mule and to run after whatever the women needed so they wouldn't have to get up so often. It would save them time, Papa had said. Even with Mama and Granda working on the corn, the boys only had to pick up the shucks every half hour or so. Mama hadn't been under the tree an hour before Jasper and Joe Ray got bored. Mama said they could go play as long as they checked back with her every few minutes.

Jasper and Joe Ray played tag out around the barn. Joe Ray was always "it" longer than Jasper 'cause Jasper was bigger and could run faster. Cindy thought they were playing hide and seek up at the barn when she went to the outhouse. But when she opened the door, her brothers pulled her inside and closed the door behind them.

"You be quiet," Jasper told Cindy, putting his hand over her mouth. "We're gonna fix your hair."

She kicked and tried to pull away, but Jasper was too strong.

"I'm gonna do it," Joe Ray said. He reached for the scissors in Jasper's hand.

"No, I am," Jasper said.

"No, me."

Joe Ray ended up using the scissors while Jasper held Cindy down. Joe Ray cut and cut and cut.

Cindy pulled a wad of silks away from the corn in her hand, remembering how she got to eat fresh corn for supper that night. Jasper and Joe Ray didn't have any. Papa had whipped them both and sent them to bed with no supper.

Cindy thought she could never forgive her brothers, but she had. She had even learned to laugh about it now that she was grown.

She smiled and shook her head, wishing she could go back to her childhood. Then she looked at Callie's fuzzy hair and laughed out loud.

Now, Cindy was a mother, and that night she did what her mama had done so many times. She boiled corn, chilled it in ice water, cut it from the cobs, and canned it in mason jars long into the night.

4

○ A Song ○

Cindy sat in the parlor sewing. She had told J.D. she had too much to do to work in the field all day, so he and Baxter had gone back by themselves after dinner. Soon as she had washed the dishes and wiped the table twice to be sure there wasn't any grease on it, she laid the material out and cut it. Then she moved Callie's cradle to the sitting room and set it in front of the rocking chair. As she sewed she rocked back and forth, pushing the baby's cradle with her foot.

Callie was going to have the prettiest christening gown of any baby the folks at Creekside Baptist had ever seen. Mama and Granda had bought the white material and lace for it that morning at Parrish's and had brought it by while she was in the field priming. She had found it between the screen door and the wood door when she came up to the house to fix dinner. She had hardly been able to get their sandwiches together, she was so excited about getting started.

She sewed along one edge of the front and back she had put together. The side seam was long. She wondered why christening gowns were made that way, longer than the baby, so that the dress trailed off toward the floor. She didn't know, but she was making Callie's that way, too. Hers was going to be made just like it had been bought ready made.

Before she died, J.D.'s mama showed her some tricks to make things look more store-bought. When J.D. brought Cindy here after they got married, Mama Rose had been here. She had treated Cindy like her own child.

That's where Callie got part of her name. "Callie" was the prettiest name Cindy could think of, so she called the baby that. But Callie's middle name was "Rose" because J.D.'s mama had been so nice to her and because she had died two months before the baby was born. It was a right pretty name, she thought, Callie Rose.

When she had finished seaming up the side, she turned the seam over on itself on the outside, topstitching it up the side like Mama Rose had told her they did in those sewing plants up north. Cindy never had asked her how she knew what they did way up there. Now she wondered about it.

Her mama sewed good, but you could still tell the clothes were homemade. Mama didn't know none of the ways they did things for store-bought clothes. Besides, Mama had always had to make most of their dresses out of flour sacks. The cloth from the flour sacks was strong and soft, and there were some pretty ones, too, like the pale blue ones, but still, everybody knew a flour-sack dress when they saw one. No getting around that.

Mama would be so proud when she saw this frock for Callie. Callie was going to have the prettiest one of any baby at Creekside Baptist. But as proud as Mama would be, Papa would be even prouder.

Papa had said over and over she had to learn how to sew good. He had even made her quit going to school so she could learn sewing and cooking.

She remembered it like it was yesterday even though it had been a year and a half ago. After Papa had told J.D. he could start calling on her, he had said she couldn't go to school no more. Said she had to learn to cook as good as he had told J.D. she could, and that she had to know how to sew good as her mama could. He hadn't even told her she had to quit school himself. He had told Mama to tell her.

Papa still thought this was where she ought to be and what she ought to be doing. Nobody would be any more tickled over how pretty she could sew than Papa when he saw the new dress on the baby at church.

Cindy turned the dress to begin the other side seam. She started humming as she sewed, pushing the cradle with her foot in time to her music.

As she kept on stitching and humming, she began to think she could hear a woman singing to what she hummed.

You get a line and I'll get a pole, honey . . .

Cindy stopped humming and listened. She could still hear it.

You get a line and I'll get a pole, babe. . .

Who could be singing? She thought of Mama Rose singing that song and talking about how her mother-in-law, Granny Spears as everybody 'round those parts called her, had loved that song and would ask her to sing it every day after she got too winded to sing much of anything herself. Cindy pushed the thought away and kept on humming.

You get a line and I'll get a pole. We'll go down to the crawdad hole, honey, baby, mine.

It was a woman's voice. At the end of the chorus, the singing stopped. Cindy sat in the rocker motionless, stilled more from wonder than fear this time. Outside, whoever or whatever was on their farm had always scared her. This was the first time it had happened right in the house, but she was not afraid. This woman's soft, feminine voice singing while she hummed was somehow comforting to her. She didn't feel alone the way she usually did when Callie napped.

Cindy started humming the same song again, but all she heard was the sound of her own voice. After she finished both side seams and started on the sleeves, she heard the spring creak on the back door.

"J.D., that you?" she called.

"Yeah."

"And me, too," Baxter yelled.

"Be right there!"

She stood up and laid the baby dress in the rocker. Callie was awake, so she lifted her out of the cradle and went to the kitchen.

"You all are back mighty early," Cindy said.

J.D. was drinking water from a mason jar. She didn't know why he insisted on doing that when they had perfectly good glasses, but he'd do it every time if she wasn't right there in the kitchen to hand him a glass.

Baxter was leaning back against the door frame, his body pushing the screen door open. Cindy saw a fly come in and land on the corner of the table.

"Me and J.D. finished barning early, so he decided for us to come on to the house stead of priming more," Baxter said.

"Thought we'd take a few hours to whittle or something," J.D. said. "Ain't had time to turn 'round good here lately for putting in 'bacca. Don't know when we've ever had a day off."

She was surprised J.D. had quit early even though he'd been working even on Sundays since the tobacco started coming off good. Baxter didn't say nothing about working on the Lord's day. He took whatever work he could get. And what could she say? Tell J.D. she was raised that it was a sin to work Sundays? All he'd say was that he worked to feed her and the baby and that she ought not to talk with her mouth full about what hours a farmer keeps.

That was one thing Papa had never done. He said he'd work like a dog every other day to the week, but he wasn't going to work on Sunday.

She could remember times when Papa would have so much to do in the field that he wouldn't come in for supper till near about midnight. But still, he wouldn't work on Sunday. And when the church doors opened on Sunday morning, Papa was there with Mama and all the younguns. Papa could've rested, but he wouldn't miss church for a thing in this world. And neither did she or the other younguns because of Papa's rule. If one of the younguns said they were sick and couldn't go to church, they stayed at home in the bed. But if they were too sick to go to church, Papa said, they were too sick to play on Sunday afternoon. They could get out of the bed to go to the outhouse and to eat, but then they had to get right back in. Going to church was something that had stayed with her, and she was glad Callie was big enough now to go.

"Well, I didn't know y'all would be back this early," Cindy said. "I ain't started supper yet, but I'll get right on it."

"Cook plenty," J.D. told her. "Baxter's gonna stay for supper tonight."

"All right," she said.

Baxter always ate breakfast and dinner with them, but most days he went on back to town before Cindy finished cooking supper. He'd say he wanted to head on before it got slam dark soon as they finished working of an evening, even though J.D. and Cindy had offered to feed him his supper, too. Cindy supposed he didn't want to wear out his welcome.

Baxter stayed at the rooming house Miss Lyda ran in town. She had a big dining room, and everybody that stayed there ate supper in it. Other people could stop by to eat, too, but not too many folks were doing that nowadays except for what few salesmen and such came through town. Money was too tight for folks 'round there to be eating at Thompson's. Miss Lyda's business had dropped way off.

"Tell you what," J.D. said. "Fry us a chicken, Cindy."

"A chicken?"

"That's what I said, ain't it?"

"Yeah. I just thought—"

"Well, don't think," he said. "I'll go kill us one."

J.D. started out the back door. Baxter stepped out on to the porch to give J.D. room to get by.

"Ain't never seen him kill a chicken when it wasn't Sunday," Cindy said out loud to herself.

Baxter stood on the porch and watched J.D. catch the chicken and wring its neck.

"That's a nice one, J.D." he said as J.D. came toward the house with the chicken. He laid it on the top step, and both of them went back into the kitchen.

"We'll wash up while you're scalding it," J.D. told Cindy.

"Mind the baby for me," she said.

In the back yard Cindy lit the wood under the black cast-iron pot and waited for the water to boil. When the water was ready, she dipped the chicken to make the feathers lose hold. Then she picked them off and dropped them on the ground.

In the kitchen Baxter bounced Callie on one knee. She was laughing at him.

"I didn't mean for you to have to watch her," Cindy said.

"Oh, it's all right," Baxter said. "I told J.D. I would. He let me go first. He's in there getting cleaned up now."

J.D. was in their bedroom at the wash stand. Cindy smiled a little to herself about it. This was the first time he'd washed in there since it turned warm in the spring. All the other nights he'd stood out there on the back porch at the pump stark naked, not a thing on between him and the Lord. She had told him she wouldn't do it for nothing in this world, but he didn't care none. Said there wasn't nobody to see him, so what did it matter. She reckoned he'd decided it mattered today being as it was broad daylight and Baxter was still here.

No, you couldn't pay her enough to wash outdoors. It just wasn't decent. Even if it was, she wouldn't give up using that wash stand for nothing. It had been Mama Rose's. J.D.'s pa had give it to her when they got married. The stand was wood, stained dark and carved 'round the edges. Mr Spears had made it himself. He'd bought the wash basin and pitcher with the little yellow flowers on them. Cindy felt special when she poured water out of that pitcher into the bowl.

Cindy floured the pieces of the chicken she'd just cut up and laid them in the hot grease. It sizzled as she put the chicken in her deepest frying pan.

Baxter was still bouncing the baby, but he was watching Cindy.

"What you smiling 'bout?" he asked her.

"Nothing," she said, laughing a little.

"Yes, you are. What?"

"J.D.," she said.

"What about him?"

"He's in there washing like he does it every day. But it's 'cause you're here. This is the first time he's washed in the house in four months."

"Naw," Baxter said. "Where's he been washing, then?"

"On the back porch," she said.

Baxter started laughing, too.

J.D. walked into the kitchen and stopped, putting his fists on the sides of his hips.

"What's so funny?" he asked Baxter.

"You out there washing on the porch naked as a jaybird."

Baxter laughed even harder and slapped the table a few times with one hand.

J.D. looked at Cindy, his eyes hard and gray. Then he turned his stare toward Baxter.

"Some things ain't none of nobody else's business," he said.

"Sorry, J.D.," Baxter said. He tried to stop laughing. "It just hit me funny's all." Then he started beating the table again, and he couldn't stop laughing.

J.D. started toward the back door, brushing his shoulder roughly against Cindy as he passed her.

"You got a lot of mouth today, ain't you?" he said.

Baxter was still laughing when J.D. pushed the door open, and turned sideways and looked at him.

"At least I wash," J.D. said.

He went on out, letting the screen door slam behind him. Cindy saw him kick a small rock on the ground in the back yard before he went into the barn.

Baxter rubbed his eyes with the back of his hand.

"I hope he ain't too mad, Cindy. I didn't mean to 'cause no trouble. I just got so tickled."

"Don't worry 'bout it," she said.

"But he's mad with you over it."

"Don't worry 'bout it, I said. It's the first time I've had a good laugh in I don't know when."

Baxter and Cindy looked at each other, and they both started laughing again.

Cindy turned back toward the counter to make biscuits. When she had finished, she put them in the oven and began slicing green tomatoes, some she had picked before they were ripe. She floured the slices and peppered them.

"Um, I love fried tomatoes," Baxter said as Cindy laid the slices in the frying pan her mama had given her.

"Me, too," she said.

She wiped her hands on her apron and turned toward the table.

"You tired of holding her yet?" she asked Baxter. She reached for Callie.

"Naw, she's fine. I'll play with her so you can finish supper."

"Well, all right," Cindy said. "She likes you. Look at her smiling. You're pretty good with a baby."

"Thanks," he said. "Had a little practice."

"That's right. One of your sisters has got a baby, ain't she?"

"Two of 'em. Sally's got a little boy and a baby girl, and Marie's got little Curtis."

"You see 'em much?"

"Did. Ain't seen 'em since I come to work here. Just have to wait till we get this 'bacca crop in."

Cindy turned the tomatoes over in the pan with a fork.

"Supper's near 'bout ready," she said. "Want me to call J.D. for you?"

"Yeah, that'll be fine. Thank you."

Baxter set Callie down on the floor. He pushed open the door and called J.D.'s name.

When J.D. came in and sat down at the table, Cindy set the chicken, tomatoes, and biscuits on the table. J.D. and Baxter fixed their plates and began to eat. Cindy put food on her plate, but she did not eat till she had fed the baby.

"This sure beats eating at the rooming house," Baxter said. "'Preciate it."

"You're mighty welcome," Cindy said. "I hear Miss Lyda's a right good cook, though. Don't know if I can top her or not."

"This here chicken can top anybody's cooking. 'Sides, it gets old quick eating there. Just ain't the same as eating at home."

"Well, you can feel at home here," Cindy said. "Ain't that right, J.D.?"

J.D. hadn't had a thing to say since they started eat.

"Yeah," he said.

"Y'all sure have been good to me," Baxter said. "The rooming house is nice and all, but it just ain't home."

"How many of y'all are staying there?" J.D. asked him.

"Well, there's me and Shorty Martin—he's hiring out on farms, too—and Freddie Nichols that works at the funeral home and Janie Elbert. Then, Miss Lyda's got one room ain't nobody staying in right now. Rents it out by the night once in awhile."

"If anybody'd told me ten years ago I'd see the day when that woman'd be running a rooming house, I'd've never believed 'em," J.D. said.

"What you mean?"

"Her and Mr Thompson had more money than anybody 'round here."

"Naw," Baxter said. "Her?"

"Yeah," Cindy said. "When I was a youngun they were rich. Bought all the finest stuff. Had that great big house all to theirselves."

"What happened?"

"Times started getting hard even for folks like them, I reckon," J.D. said. "Thompson went through near 'bout every dollar his old man had left him, buying this and buying that, and then the little barber shop he tended to be running went under. Had to let the man he had cutting hair for him go. Found him dead that same day in his shop."

"Killed hisself?"

"Well, they say it was heart trouble."

"Reckon if he did, nobody wanted to tell Miss Lyda that," Baxter said. "She's such a nice old lady."

"Proves you can teach an old dog new tricks," J.D. said.

"What's that s'posed to mean?"

"Used to be an ole bat."

"Naw," Baxter said.

"Yeah, she was, too," Cindy said. "Felt herself too good for folks."

"Uppity," J.D. said.

"Well, I'll be," Baxter said. "I'd've never thought it. I reckon money can change things."

"Yeah," Cindy said, laughing.

"What's the matter with you?" Baxter asked.

"My brothers used to call her 'the ole crow.' One time when we were younguns, Jasper and Joe Ray and some other boys were setting on the back row in church. She was setting right in front of 'em. Willie Crawford dared 'em to pour water down her back."

"And they did it?" Baxter asked. He took another piece of chicken from the plate in the middle of the table.

"Joe Ray did. Jasper chickened out and wouldn't do it. Told Joe Ray Papa was gonna beat him to death, but Joe Ray didn't pay him no mind. Sneaked out and got a dipper full."

"And just dumped it on her, like that?"

"Well, not all at once. Least that's what Jasper said. Said after everybody got to sweating and fanning, Joe Ray dripped the water on her back a little at a time so she wouldn't notice. Done all right, too, till Junior Prescott bumped him and the rest of the water spilled on her hair."

J.D. and Baxter laughed.

"You ought to have heard the fuss she made 'bout him messing up her hairdo. She never did like younguns noway. She wasn't 'bout to just let it go by. The preacher even stopped the sermon for her."

"Some folks," Baxter said.

"I won't never forget her grabbing up them combs that fell out of her hair and storming out of the church-house like somebody had set her on fire."

"Oh, I ought not to laugh so much when I'm this full," Baxter said.

"You 'bout ready to do some whittling?" J.D. asked him.

"Yeah, maybe you can teach me something new."

"Well, I don't know 'bout all that," J.D. said.

Baxter and J.D. left the table, Baxter pushing his chair under before leaving the kitchen.

"Come on up here to the front," J.D. said. He led the way from the kitchen into the hallway that led to the main part of the house.

"You close this in yourself?" Baxter asked him as they left the kitchen.

A lot of folks were building their houses different nowadays. Didn't seem to be nowhere near as scared of fire as they used to be. Built the kitchen right in with the rest of the house now. Cindy reckoned that them gas stoves people were buying didn't never throw no sparks.

She put Callie on the floor to play, heated water in a kettle on the stove and poured it into the dishpan with the cooler water. She washed the dishes quickly but carefully, dried them, and put them back in the cabinets. Then she swept the floor.

When she finished in the kitchen, she took Callie up to the parlor where J.D. and Baxter were whittling. She laid the baby in the cradle and sat down in the chair, holding the christening gown in her lap. She watched them for a minute as they whittled, letting the wood shavings drop onto the floor. Tomorrow she would take the braided rug Mama Rose had made outside and hang it across the clothesline where she could beat it with the broom to get the shavings out.

Cindy gave Callie a string of emptied wooden spools she had tied together with cotton twine. Callie, lying on her back, shook the spools and smiled at the rattle they made when they bumped together.

Cindy threaded her needle and continued working on the christening gown.

Baxter stopped his whittling and looked at the baby playing, then at J.D.

"How's that bird coming, J.D.?" he asked him.

"All right, I reckon. Hard piece of wood, though."

"Mine, too.

Baxter laid his knife and half-finished figure on the small table side his chair. He rubbed his hands together palm to palm.

"What you making over there?" he asked Cindy.

"A christening gown for the baby," she said.

"Oh, bet that's gonna look mighty nice on her," Baxter said.

"For what?" J.D. asked her.

"You know," she said. "Said I'd start taking her to church soon. I'm able to go back, and she's big enough to ride in the wagon if'n I hold her. Needs a little white frock to wear to be baptized in when we take her Sunday."

"Ain't no sense in it. Ain't doing nothing but wasting money."

Cindy kept on sewing. She didn't look up at him.

"What'd you do, sneak off to Parrish's to get that white stuff when we were working?"

"No."

"How'd you get it then?"

Cindy was embarrassed. She could feel J.D.'s eyes on her. She knew that Baxter was looking at her, too, but his gaze didn't go through her like J.D.'s did. She rubbed the sole of her bare foot against the oval rug that covered the middle of the floor between all the chairs. The braiding scratched and tickled her foot.

"How?" J.D. asked her again.

"Mama and Granda brung it to me."

"They pay for it?" he asked.

"Yeah."

"Ain't I told you we don't take nothing from nobody?"

She kept on sewing, still not looking up at him or Baxter.

"Ain't I?"

"Didn't take nothing," Cindy said. "They brung it for the baby. Was a present."

"I don't care what you call it," he said. "She don't need it, noway, just to wear one time."

"I'll let her wear it some more. Outgrowing her clothes fast as I can make 'em as it is. She can use something else."

She could tell J.D was mad even if he hadn't said a word. He let out a long, loud breath through his nose. He sounded a lot like a bull, the way he always did when he got mad. She laid the little dress down on her lap and looked up. Baxter was watching her. They looked at each other, and she knew her pain was coming right out of her eyes without her saying a word.

Baxter picked up the piece of wood he'd been carving. He rolled it 'round in his hands.

"Which Sunday y'all gonna do it?" Baxter asked after awhile. "Wouldn't mind being there myself. She's gonna look mighty cute."

"This Sunday if I can finish it in time. I reckon I can," Cindy said.

She heard J.D. blowing out his breath again.

"Just carrying on foolishness," he said. "Just take the youngun there and do it. Ain't got to have nothing fancy for the Lord to take you."

"Oh, come on, J.D.," Baxter said. "Let the youngun have a little frock. Your baby ain't christened but one time."

J.D. looked at Cindy, his forehead slightly wrinkled.

"I need you to work," he said.

"I'll work," she said.

"Yeah, like you did today. Quit at dinner time much as there is to be done?"

Baxter looked at Cindy, then at J.D.

"I'll work extra this week," he told J.D.

"I can't pay you no more than I already am. Can't have you working over," J.D. said.

"It's all right. I don't expect no more pay."

J.D. glared at him and then at Cindy, his hair sticking up like it did so often.

Cindy looked up at Baxter and smiled slightly. It was so nice of him to help her out like that so she could finish the baby's dress.

J.D. and Baxter went back to whittling. J.D. struck his knife against the wood with rough, jerky motions. He'd never come out with anything that looked decent, working like that.

Cindy kept on with her sewing. J.D. wouldn't mind her sewing for a boy, she thought. He sure didn't mind her sewing and fixing clothes for him. Men wore practical clothes, things to work in, J.D. always said, but women spent too much time worrying about frillly stuff on theirs. Women just wanted to show off with all that mess, he said. He was only half right. She didn't want to show off, but she wanted her baby to have the prettiest christening gown ever. After all, what was wrong with a mama wanting nice things for her baby?

She wondered if he would ever love Callie like he would have loved a boy.

5

○ Sam ○

Cindy strained the water from the cabbage she had boiled for dinner. She put a saucer on top of the cooked leaves and pressed down on it, mashing the cabbage so that the rest of the water would drain through the holes in the aluminum strainer. When she was sure she had all the water out, she chopped the cabbage up fine.

She took up the fatback from the frying pan and spooned some of the grease from it into the cabbage, stirring the cabbage and grease together. Then she cut some of the strips of fatback into little pieces. She mixed the pieces in with the cabbage and ate a few pieces of the hard, crunchy skin. She never put in the skin. Next, she peeled and washed some Irish potatoes. While they were cooking, she sliced the tomatoes. She had everything on the table when J.D. and Baxter came in for dinner. She could tell they were both real hungry by the way they looked at the food and how fast they started grabbing biscuits and piling food on their plates.

They had been hoeing corn all morning. J.D. had said they would do that for a couple of days to let the next leaves up the tobacco stalks get good and ripe.

Cindy looked at their hands. The brownish calluses made them look kind of dirty even though they'd washed up out at the pump. She had red places on her hands where she'd had blisters that popped and were just now healing. Papa said that was one way you could always tell a farmer. First you looked at his neck. If you couldn't see the back of his neck, look at his hands. For sure they'd be tough from hoes and plows and stuff, he said.

Baxter took two slices from the plate of tomatoes. "I seen a fella eat more of these here things last night than I've ever seen anybody eat in my life," he said.

"Really?" J.D. asked. "Who?"

"This fella that come to the rooming house. Come there night 'fore last, but I didn't see him till yestiddy 'cause I was here the other night. Staying in that room down the hall that's been empty. Anyhow, all I got to say is that he can hide some 'matoes."

"Maybe he ain't never seen none before," J.D. said, grinning a little.

"He's had some all right. Miss Lyda said he stayed there 'bout this same time last year, and he near 'bout ate her out of house and home. Got him a little bit of a pot belly to show for it, too."

Cindy alternated between giving Callie bites of food and eating her own dinner.

"Where 'bouts is he from?" J.D. asked.

"Says he was raised in Memphis, but he don't stay 'round there much no more. Just goes back now and again visiting family, you know, still got his mama there and all. Rest of the time he's traveling 'round selling shoes, mostly to stores, but he goes 'round to some houses, too, if he hears anybody wants to buy any."

Cindy swallowed her food wrong and almost choked. She coughed till her eyes watered.

"You all right?" J.D. asked her.

"Yeah," she said. "Just need to drink a little water."

She saw that Baxter was looking at her, too, and she was embarrassed. She picked up her glass and drank some water. J.D. and Baxter started back eating when they saw she was all right.

"Well, we don't want no shoes," J.D. said to Baxter. "Can't afford no shoes. He needn't come knocking on this door."

"'Magine it's the same with everybody, J.D. A shoe salesman's gonna be mighty hard pressed 'round here."

"You better believe it," J.D. said.

"If he does sell anything, it'll be work boots."

"Won't be no Sunday ones, that's for sure."

Baxter and J.D. went on talking about how bad things were, how the salesman wasn't going to sell nothing, and all. Cindy sat there thinking about what Baxter had said. The shoe salesman had been there before. He had a little too much 'round the middle and loved a tomato better than anything. She knew him. She knew him.

After dinner when J.D. and Baxter had gone back to their hoeing, Cindy washed up the dishes and went outside to wash clothes. She worked on the back porch so she'd be right next to the pump, but she let Callie play on a blanket on the ground below so she wouldn't fall down the steps.

She rubbed one of J.D.'s white shirts against the washboard. It was filthy on the inside where the collar met the yolk. His light shirts were always nasty there from the sweat and the dirt. She'd told him to save it for Sunday, but sometimes in the mornings he'd grab the best one he had and go out to work in it. She had even tried putting it in a different drawer from the rest of the shirts so he'd have one that wasn't stained or picked or thin from all the scrubbing. She looked down at Callie and saw that the baby was at the edge of the quilt. Cindy put back the shirt and went down the steps to move Callie back to the middle of the blanket. "Now you stay right there where you won't get so dirty and where the ants won't tote you off," she told the baby.

When Cindy went back up on the porch, she picked up the shirt she'd been washing and started scrubbing a stain on the sleeve. No way she could get that spot clean. It must be grease, ground in deep and black as the ace of spades. J.D. must have caught it 'round the wheel and axle of the tobacco truck. A working man didn't mind a little dirt, he always said.

She thought about Sam's shirts, white as snow and crisp with starch. She had smelled the cleanness of the starch when she'd seen him in the store, when he'd gone to her church that Sunday, and when he'd met her that day outside the schoolhouse. That was the last time she'd seen him, but she could still smell that starch.

She went into the kitchen to the cabinet where she kept the soap. She pulled a chair from the table up to the counter and stood on it, taking the box of Argo from the top shelf. After she pushed the chair back under the table, she shook a few lumps of the old starch into a small pan. She dissolved the starch with a little of the water she had left in the kettle from when she heated up the dish water. She breathed in deep, taking in the clean excitement of the starch.

When she went back out onto the porch, Callie wasn't on the blanket. Cindy felt like her heart was going to drop right down into her stomach. Quickly, she set the pan of starch on the porch, a little of it spilling over the side and running along the floor board to the edge of the porch, and ran down the steps to look for the baby. She found her just under the porch. Reaching under like she did for potatoes or wood, she pulled Callie out from under the house, starch dripping on the back of the baby's head from the porch. Cindy took a rag from her apron pocket and wiped the starch off Callie's head. Then she brushed the dirt off the baby's knees with her hand and put her back on the quilt. Her heart was still beating hard.

"I should've known not to leave you for a minute."

She starched the shirts she'd already scrubbed in the foot-tub, wrung them out, and pinned them on the line so they could be drying. After they dried she would sprinkle them down just a little, let them set awhile, and then iron them. While the shirts were on the line, she went on washing the rest of the clothes.

Cindy kept a close watch on the baby to be sure she didn't get under the house again. Liable to be a snake up under there laying in the shade where it was cool. Or she might turn some of the wood over on herself. Some folks let little younguns play up under houses, specially when it was hot and they were going to get out and play in the dirt anyhow, but she wasn't about to do it. It was too dangerous. Anything could be up under that house and you not know it. She didn't want nothing to happen to Callie.

Some days she thought she'd go crazy around there if she didn't have Callie. Before the crop started coming in, when J.D. would go to the field, she had the baby to be at least some company to her. She remembered how it was before Callie was born, after Mama Rose had died. Some days when J.D. was gone, she felt like she was the only person left in the world, like God had come and taken everybody up to heaven but her. Even when J.D. came in it was better. He just wasn't much of a talker with her. He'd eat his supper and sit on the front porch just staring at the dirt road or whittling if it wasn't storming. If it was, he'd sit in the parlor. She'd have the kitchen to straighten up and more housework to do. Come dark, they'd go to bed together but still not talking much, and start all over in the morning. Now she had Callie, and she wasn't about to let nothing happen to that baby.

She looked down at Callie, and she felt bad that J.D. didn't want her.

She had not wanted a baby either, but then she never had planned on getting married or being here. She'd just wanted to teach school. She remembered how it used to upset Mama and Papa so bad that she didn't want the same things they wanted for her, that she didn't want to give them grandchildren or get married or run a busy house. She had not wanted J.D. either. She didn't regret feeling like that one bit. But Papa and Mama had thought he was the one for her from the start. She could still remember clear as a bell what Mama had said to her the day after Papa had told J.D. he could marry her. She and Mama were sitting in the kitchen waiting for the stove to get hot so they could cook. Mama had started in on her and wouldn't let up.

"You know, Cindy," Mama had said, "J.D. is a right nice fella."

"Mama."

"Well, he is, Cindy. Your pa's thinking he'll make you a good husband."

"No," she said.

"Just give it a chance," Mama said.

"Ain't no chance to give, Mama."

"Why not?"

"Cause there ain't. I can't be marrying nobody."

"But you've got to, Cindy. Every woman's got to have a husband, somebody to look after her, somebody to give her children and be a daddy."

"I don't want none of that."

"What's wrong with it? What's wrong with you?"

"Nothing's wrong with me. Ain't nothing wrong with having a dream, and mine's being a teacher."

"But it's a dream that can't come true, Cindy."

"It will," she had insisted.

"No, it won't."

"Mama."

"And what're we s'posed to tell folks when they start asking how come you're an old maid?"

Cindy had bitten her lip, trying not to cry when Mama said that.

"That's exactly what you're gonna be. And not no old maid school teacher neither. Just plain old maid. Just hanging 'round here for me and your pa to look after all your life."

"Mama!"

"Face it, Cindy. You gotta get yourself a husband 'fore you get too old. Gotta get him while you're young and purty."

She remembered how she had not said anything, concentrating on not crying. Mama had kept on.

"And what about babies, Cindy? Don't you want younguns, grandyounguns? You need somebody to look after you when you're old."

"I don't want none."

"Don't say that. You don't mean it, and folks'll be talking 'bout you. There's something wrong with a girl that don't want no babies."

"No there ain't, Mama."

"But why, Cindy? Why don't you want the things every other girl wants?"

"'Cause I want to teach, Mama, and you can't teach with a husband and babies."

"Oh, Cindy, listen to yourself. Listen to what you're saying. A mama is a teacher. A mama is the best kind of teacher there is. Who else is gonna learn your younguns their manners and tell 'em to go to church and show 'em how to button their shirts? Ain't nobody gonna do all that but a mama, Cindy."

"You're just trying to make me feel better 'bout getting married."

"Well, what if I am? It oughtta make you see that getting married ain't all as bad as you make it out to be."

"Well, it don't, Mama. I still got my dream, and nothing you say is gonna change it."

"Dreams get broke, Cindy. 'Round here, we don't have no big dreams. We can't afford 'em. Just like they don't have that fine china on them big ships you read about. Hit rough water, and they get broke. Same thing, Cindy."

She knew Mama had meant well, and Papa, too. She had heard Mama tell Granda so. "Don't want to see her hurt," Mama had said to Granda. "Don't know which is worse—telling her that farmers' daughters ain't never no more than farmers' wives or letting her be an old maid with nobody to look after her."

Cindy scrubbed a pair of J.D.'s overalls against the washboard as hard as she could. The last of the threads gave way. She had worn a hole in them. She'd patch them before she put them in the bedroom for him to wear.

She looked out across the yard and the field to the trees, as far as she could see. A farmer's wife. That's all she was.

She brought her eyes down and looked at Callie. If she had to be a farmer's wife, this baby was her one bright spot, she supposed. When she had found out that she was going to have a baby, she wanted that baby. It was going to be her baby, and it belonged with her. Now, she loved her Callie better than anything in this world, and she wished that J.D. did, too. But he never even picked her up unless he had to. Never picked her up just to play awhile like

Cindy did. As long as he put food on the table and kept a roof over their heads, he thought that was enough. He just didn't see what she saw, that a baby needed touching and holding and loving, things besides just food.

Callie was not going to have to do what she'd had to do. She meant it. No matter what she had to do, Callie wasn't going to be like her. She looked at the baby. Callie was still sitting up on the middle of the blanket looking back at her, smiling.

"You're not going to be a farmer's wife," she said. "I promise you you're not going to be."

Callie sat there wobbling from side to side a little, smiling at her.

A gust of wind blew across the back yard, making a long, sad moan as it passed through the holes in the pipe where the rain water drained down from the top of the house.

"She's not going to be a farmer's wife," Cindy said into the wind.

The wind blew harder, and the moaning from the pipe was louder. It was so sad, and it went on and on and on.

6

○ The Rain ○

Cindy put the pan of biscuits she'd just made in the oven. She broke some eggs into a frying pan with a little bit of bacon grease and left the pan on the counter. Then she went to the bedroom and picked up Callie.

"Breakfast's almost ready," she told J.D.

She went back to the kitchen, taking the baby with her. She wiped the sleep from under the baby's eyes with her thumb as she walked. After she changed Callie's diaper, she set her on the floor so she could finish cooking. Callie crawled to the table and pulled herself upright, holding on to the table leg for support.

Cindy set the frying pan on the stove and beat the eggs with a wood spoon to scramble them. She turned to look at Callie and saw that she was trying to stand up. She was wobbling even though she held tight to the table leg.

"Girl, you're gonna fall and bust your head."

Callie laughed at her and let go of the leg, sitting down hard on her padding of diaper. She blinked her eyes and then opened them wide with surprise when she hit the floor. Cindy was surprised that she didn't cry. She couldn't help laughing at the look on Callie's face. "Well, I told you so," she said to the baby. "Better that end than the other, I reckon."

Cindy kept on stirring the eggs, scraping the end of the spoon against the bottom of the pan where the eggs were trying to stick. She took the pan off the stove when the eggs were done, holding the handle with a rag she had wrapped 'round it to keep from burning herself. As she was raking some of the eggs onto each plate with the wood spoon, Baxter came up on the back porch and knocked on the door.

"Come on in," she told him.

"Morning," he said, closing the door behind him.

"Morning," she said. "Hungry?"

"I'm always hungry. You know that."

Cindy laughed. She set the empty frying pan in the dishpan of water so the pieces of egg left in the pan wouldn't get hard.

"Right chilly out there this morning to be this time of year," Baxter said.

"Yeah, it was when I put the baby's diaper out on the porch a while ago," she said. "Reckon it's the rain."

It had started drizzling late the afternoon before—not a hard rain, just enough to get you wet—and it hadn't stopped since. It would do the crops good, though, especially the corn. A good steady rain that had time to soak in was a lot better for the crops than hard, fast rain that ran right off into the ditches before it had time to do any good. J.D. said he hoped they'd get a plenty of that kind of rain this year. Said if they got enough water they'd make a good corn crop this year. Water could make or break the corn. Without it, the kernels would be small, not fully developed—nubby, Papa called it. But enough water could make you a bumper crop, and they sure needed one now. Everybody was hoping for the same thing.

J.D. came into the kitchen. He still didn't comb his hair of a morning even though Baxter was there and had combed his. She had thought that might shame him into doing a little something to himself when he got up mornings, but it hadn't. His hair looked like weeds on the edge of a woods fire—still standing and singed black, but not burnt slam up.

"Morning, J.D.," Baxter said. "We still gonna work this morning?"

"Yeah," J.D. said. "Can't let a little rain keep me from it. Got too much to do. Ain't lightning or nothing, just raining. Just get wet is all."

After they ate, J.D. went to the bedroom to get his hat so the water wouldn't run in his eyes so bad he couldn't see. Cindy started getting the dishes off the table and putting them in the dishpan.

"Y'all still got company at the rooming house?" she asked Baxter.

"Yeah. Don't know why, though. Ain't heard him say much 'bout selling nothing."

"Maybe he just wants to stay put in one place a while."

"Don't know. Mentioned something 'bout having a friend here. Said he might look him up while he's here. Don't know who he is, though."

Cindy wiped the table with the wet dishrag. She would not go with them to the field even though she had finished the dress for Callie the day before. She couldn't take the baby to the field and leave her in the pen while it was raining. She would have to stay at the house.

J.D. came back through the kitchen with his hat. "You got a hat?" he asked Baxter.

"Yeah, left it and my coat on the porch."

He had walked back to town to the rooming house the day before without either after the rain started.

"I'll be in the corn," J.D. said as he opened the back door. He didn't look at her, but she knew he was talking to her.

"See you at dinner," Baxter said.

"Don't get marred up to your eyeballs," Cindy said.

Cindy went over and made sure the back door was closed good after they left, not wanting the cool dampness to get inside.

She washed the rest of the dishes and swept the floor. She needed to mop, but there wasn't no need to do it now. J.D. and Baxter'd be tracking in mud at dinner, and she'd bring it in too after she fed the chickens. If it stopped raining, she could mop tomorrow.

She carried Callie up to the parlor and set her on the floor. From the closet in the corner behind the front door she got a rag and started dusting the furniture. She was careful to get between all the spokes on the back of the rocking chairs and to be sure the rockers and rails at the bottom were clean, too. When she was a youngun, Mama would make her go back over the rocking chairs again if she didn't get them clean.

Back then, she thought she had to do a lot, that she had too many chores to do 'round the house. Now she knew what Mama had been doing all those years. It wasn't easy tending to a baby, cooking three meals a day, keeping the house clean, washing all the clothes, tending to a garden and chickens. She just didn't know about all that till she had it to do.

She wouldn't be so busy, she supposed, if she was a teacher. She could go to school and teach. When she went home, she'd just have a room or two at some place like Miss Lyda's to look after. Nothing like a whole house and a family to care for. She looked at Callie, and she knew she wouldn't trade her for a thing in this world, but there were those days when she couldn't help thinking about how things would be if she had been able to follow her heart.

She could have had her own job and her own money, and nobody to answer to but herself. She wouldn't have been here in this house on this farm where the woods cross the road and the woods on the other side of the fields and back by the creek were as far as you could see. Woods every whichway you looked like the fences around a fort.

What would it be like to ride in a car for miles on end, ride and ride and ride till you found that place where the sky meets the ground? Sam knew.

She hadn't wanted to marry anybody, but sometimes she wished she'd run off with Sam when he asked her to. He had said she could go with him, and maybe she should have done just that. She'd told him there was no way under the sun Papa and Mama would let her go with him, and he'd said she could just up and run off. But she couldn't stand to hurt them like that. Now look where that had gotten her—here. Having to marry J.D. was the thanks she got for doing like she ought to.

When she finished her dusting, she put Callie down for a nap and went out onto the front porch to sit in the swing. It had been so long since she'd done that, just sit on the porch and swing. It was still raining, and she watched the drops come down and hit the ground with flat little thuds. She loved to watch it rain. She had loved it ever since she was a little girl, when she would sneak out on the porch when Mama said not to, just so she could watch the rain. She liked its quietness, and she liked how loud it could be on the tin roof of the house. She liked the way she felt closer to God when it rained and how she could sit on the porch or stand at the window and feel safe and warm and dry when everything else was wet. As long as it didn't come up a bad storm, she was glad to see the rain.

J.D. hated rain, hated the gray sky. She never had told him about the dark blues and purples you could see up there when it rained if you'd just look. That was her secret.

She looked off down the road to where it passed through the trees of the 'cosin. She couldn't see a thing past there. So she listened, listened for the sound of a motor that she knew would not, could not come. The salesman wanted to look up his friend, Baxter said. He had called her his friend. He had called her his friend that day they sat in his car and he offered to take her away and never bring her back. But she knew he would not come. If he asked about her, for sure whoever he asked would tell him how to get to their place, but they'd tell him, too, that she was now Mrs J.D. Spears. Then he would not come.

But she wanted to see him, talk to him, ask him to tell her again about the places he had been. She could show him her Callie, too, tell him that it wasn't all bad that she had not gone with him, that she had a gem for keeps no matter how hard the mining.

She would find a way to see him. She would find a reason to go to town as soon as it stopped this raining. J.D. had been going to town on Saturday mornings before the crop started coming in. She had even gone with him sometimes before she found out she was expecting. But now he didn't have time to go regular. Just went when they couldn't do without any longer. To be sure she could find something they were out of, something they needed. She'd tell him that since the baby was big enough to ride, she'd hitch up the wagon and go herself to save him some time.

She got up from the swing to go inside. She'd have to be sure she had a decent dress clean. She wished it would stop all this raining.

When she opened the front door, the rocking chair over by the back wall of the parlor was rocking a little like somebody had just got up from it, setting it in motion. That was the oldest chair in the house, the one Mama Rose had always sat in.

Mama Rose said that chair was already there, and well worn, when she came to the 'cosin. Every woman of this house must have sat in that chair. And now it was rocking by itself. Couldn't've been the wind. She had the doors and windows closed. Cindy walked through the hall to the kitchen to see if somebody had come and gone through the back door, but she didn't see anybody in the back yard at all.

When she went back up to the parlor, the chair was still. She looked around, but nothing was out of place.

"Anybody in here?" she asked.

Nobody answered, so she sat down in the chair herself. It started rocking again, but she was not pushing against the floor with her feet. She wasn't moving at all. Cindy got up from the chair, and it was still again. Then, it rocked just a little, and stopped.

Cindy went over to the bedroom door and opened it enough to look in to see if Callie was all right. The baby was still asleep, breathing in her tiny way like J.D. After she saw the baby was fine, Cindy went back to the chair and sat in it again.

She pulled her legs up into the chair, crossing them and tucking them under her dress so that she was sitting like the books said the Indians sat in their tepees. Then she was careful to be real still. She sat there a while, thinking of going to town and what she might wear. On the roof the raindrops beat harder, faster, till all she could hear was the roar of water on tin. She sat there under the roaring till she was sleepy. Slowly, rhythmically, the chair began to rock again, rocking easy, easy, easy. And she let the chair that belonged to the women of the house rock her to sleep.

Back and forth, back and forth. All her life was a rocking chair. Back and forth, back and forth Mama had rocked her. Forward and back, forward and back, then back, back, back went her hope till the chair near about turned over. Back and forth she had rocked on the porch when J.D. came to call. Rock-a-bye, go to sleep, back and forth with Callie. Back and forth, back and forth. All her life was a rocking chair.

Callie was crying from the bedroom, ready to get up. Cindy realized she was still, no longer rocking, and that she had been asleep. She got up from the chair and went into the bedroom to tend to the baby.

Back in the parlor, she rocked Callie back and forth, remembering in pieces and flashes what she had just dreamed. She thought of Mama and how she used to rock her when she was a youngun if she was sick. Didn't matter how much her Mama had to do, how many younguns she had to tend to, she always did first for the one that was sick. She wondered if it came out of love, sorrow that a youngun was sick, or if it came out of the fear of losing one. The hardest thing in the world for a woman to bear was losing a youngun, her own flesh and blood.

She thought of rocking on the porch when she was a girl. She would sit on the porch for as long as they'd let her, sometimes till after dark when they'd make her go in. In the summertime she'd finish up her chores after supper and go out there and read or watch the sun go down. She'd sneak out there when it rained even though Mama said she'd get chilled and catch a cold, just so she could watch it falling.

She rocked on the porch, too, when Papa let J.D. come to call on her, Sundays after church. She could remember that first time he came over and how outdone he'd been that she wouldn't sit with him in the swing. Served him right. She hadn't wanted him to come nohow, and she told Mama so. But Mama said Papa had already said he could come calling, and Mama wasn't about to go through the embarrassment of telling him he couldn't. Besides, Mama said, she thought it was time to find her a husband, and J.D. was as good as any.

In church that Sunday she'd opened her eyes during the prayer and seen him looking at her. She'd told Granda about it, too, thinking maybe Granda would tell Mama and Papa he didn't have no manners. But Granda laughed at her and said she wouldn't have known he was looking at her during the prayer if she hadn't been looking at him.

When Mama had put her finest Sunday dinner—fried chicken, potato salad, and string beans that she told J.D. Cindy had cooked all by herself—on the table, Cindy had piled up her plate and eaten all she could, wanting him to think he couldn't afford to feed her. But that didn't do no good, neither. All he said was that he liked to see a girl who would eat enough to stay strong.

And then she and J.D. had sat on the porch all Sunday evening. She'd offered to help with the dishes, but Mama wouldn't hear of it with J.D. there to call on her. Papa had told them they could sit on the porch a spell and talk, so that's where they'd gone. And that's when J.D. sat in the swing and patted the spot beside him with his hand. She sat down in one of the chairs and rocked as hard as she could, and she could tell he didn't like it none. Served him right. He was just like every other man. Thought that just because he'd asked her papa could he come a calling and just because Papa had said it was all right, that she had to like it or at least act like she did. But she showed him a thing or two. He sat there and whistled like he'd won a prize somewhere, but she could've told him different. He couldn't carry a tune in a bucket. And then he tried talking to her some, but she didn't say one word to him unless he asked her a question. She was still rocking hard as she could go when he told her folks goodbye and rode his horse off down the road and out of sight.

And she was rocking hard now, she realized, so hard she almost bumped the chair against the wall behind her.

After rocking Callie a little longer and singing her "Oh, Suzanna," Cindy headed for the kitchen to fix some dinner. It wasn't time for dinner yet, but she knew J.D. and Baxter would be on in with it raining so hard. It wasn't showing no signs of letting up.

Out at the pump, she washed some of the squash she'd picked a few days before. It was raining so hard the pipes couldn't hold all the water running off the roof. It poured off the edges of the house so fast that it hit the soaked ground and splattered up on the porch where she was standing.

Cindy carried the squash into the kitchen, carefully stepping around Callie. She sliced the squash thin into the frying pan. Then she peeled and sliced onions, dropping the cut rings on top of the squash. She poured a little water into the pan and set it on the stove.

She went to the back door, opened it and stood there looking through the screen at the rain while she waited for the squash to start cooking. Out at the chicken pen everything was still, quiet. She couldn't see a one of the chickens, but she knew where they were. Most of them were up in the nest boxes shrunk back in there as far as they could go to keep from getting wet. A few were under the barrel J.D. had buried partway in the ground, three-fourths of it left to make a little shelter above the ground for the chickens to get under. She had put straw in there so it would be warm like the nests. Sometimes she would push the straw back a little and put some cracked corn just under the edge when it was raining like this and wouldn't let up. They might not come out and eat in the rain, but then they just might, and she couldn't stand for them to be hungry and hunting food and not have none.

Near the back of the barn in the split rail fence, she could see the mule and J.D.'s horse and Baxter's. Baxter had ridden his to work this morning the way he did about half the time.The rest of the time he walked. On those days when he rode, J.D. let him put Strawberry down there with old Jack and Nellie. The animals had everything they needed back there—a fenced space big enough to walk in, sweet molasses-smelling feed inside and hay if they needed it, big water trough, and a big enough space in the barn with a door cut wide so they could walk in and out as they pleased. But they were standing out in the rain as if they didn't know they were wet. They beat all she'd ever seen. She'd even been out there many a time when it was raining and got wet herself leading old Jack and Nellie in to be sure they knew they could get out of the weather.

But she'd learned better than to even try anymore. They were just going to walk right back out in it as soon as she left the barn. When she was a youngun she never had known about horses doing that because they stayed right behind the barn where you couldn't see them unless you went down there. But here she could see them out on one side of the barn, and it always bothered her somehow about them standing in the rain. That was just their nature, she reckoned, to stand under the shower of rain with their hind ends turned toward the wind. Maybe at least the rain would wash the dust off their hides.

Sometimes when she'd pet them dust would rise up out of their coats in little clouds, and her hand would be right gritty. Old Jack couldn't help it none about the dust. She felt like that, too, some days after she'd been in the field and the wind had blown the plowed dirt all over her. She had even seen the time she could taste the dirt, feel the grit in her mouth when it was dry. But Nellie was a different story. She'd have her spells where she'd just lay down right in the loosest dirt she could find in the fence and roll from side to side, her legs up in the air. She was a good-natured thing, so that must be her way of playing, Cindy thought. Either that or it eased some urge. Sometimes when she itched Nellie would stand in the doorway between the barn and the fence pressed up against the frame. She'd rub back and forth scratching herself.

Cindy thought that if she saw Zeb Smith at church or town, she'd think to ask him if all the horses at his stable did the same things. If anybody would know, it would be Mr Zeb. He'd put up more horses than she'd ever see, even Baxter's Strawberry. Janie's horse, too. Never had turned a animal away that needed a place to stay, he'd tell you in a heartbeat. He was proud of that. If he didn't have the room, he'd make the room. Kept horses for everybody in town that needed a place to put one. Took them in for a night or two for folks just passing through. He'd even gone clear out there to Bright's crossroads to get Granda's horse and take him back to town that time she was so sick and had to stay with Mama and Papa for a while. Papa could've got him and tended to him fine, but Mr Zeb had sent word that he'd tend to the horse and wouldn't charge Granda not one penny being as she was sick. Least he could do for her and the horse, he said.

On the stove the water in the pan was bubbling. Cindy stirred the squash and onions from the bottom, making sure they weren't trying to stick. She got out the flour and lard and made up her biscuits.

After she put the biscuits in the oven, she went back to the screen door and stood there looking out. Water was running cross the back yard where the ground was sloped, running right through the outhouse—through the gap between the bottom of the wall and the ground on one side and out the smaller crack on the other side. She'd have to tell J.D. to dig a trench to carry the water the other way before the whole thing gave way and fell down. That's all they needed was for the outhouse to fall in. Then they'd have to use the slop jar in the bedroom all the time, not just in the night, till J.D. could get a new one built. She'd have to tell J.D. to dig that trench quick.

She saw J.D. and Baxter out past the barn, coming this way. Didn't surprise her none. No way they could keep on hoeing with it raining like this. The water was running across the field where they were trying to chop by now, she reckoned. It was the lowest field on the farm, the one going down on both sides toward the middle. J.D. had helped his pa dig many a trench out there, she'd heard him say, to let the water out from between the rows so it would go into the ditches.

They walked slow, not a bit of hurry about them. Wasn't no need. They were done wet, and they were early for dinner. Wasn't no need at all for them to hurry. They'd be tickled when they got up here and found out she'd done cooked them some dinner.

She folded a dish towel in half and then again so that it was four layers thick, and set the sizzling pan of squash on it in the middle of the table. She did the same for the pan of biscuits. Then she set the table so everything would be ready when J.D. and Baxter came in. Seeing that Callie had crawled over too close to the door, she picked the baby up and moved her to the other side of the kitchen.

"You can't be right in the door," she told the baby. "They'll step on you trying to get in. Set right here just a minute, and Mama'll feed you."

She could see Baxter and J.D. through the window. On the back porch they took off their hats. Baxter took off his coat and hung it on a nail against the back wall of the house. J.D. took off the flannel shirt he'd worn over the short-sleeve one and wrung it out. He laid it in the chair. Both of them pulled off their boots and left them beside the door.

"Y'all drowned yet?" Cindy asked them when they came inside.

"Would be for much," Baxter said. "It's raining cats and dogs out there."

"Field flooding?" she asked.

"Some," J.D. said. "Hoping it'll run off."

"Why don't y'all put on some dry clothes before you eat?"

"B'lieve I will," Baxter said. "Least I'll feel better for a while, till we go out again."

He kept him an extra set of clothes in the chifferobe up there in the spare room, the room that used to be Mama Rose's.

"You gone change your clothes, J.D.?" he asked.

"Yeah, coming out of this shirt for sure."

J.D. unbuttoned his shirt and took it off right there in the kitchen, dropping it on the floor near the door going into the hall.

"You starch this shirt? It stinks," he told her.

He went on up toward the front of the house, and Baxter followed him.

Cindy poured water in the glasses she had put on the table. She picked up the baby and sat down. While she was waiting for them to come back, she put a spoon of squash on her plate, picking out soft pieces of the squash but no onions and putting them in the baby's mouth with her fingers.

Baxter came back to the kitchen before J.D. He sat down at the table across from her, leaving the place at the end for J.D. He winked at Callie and made funny faces at her, and she grinned at him.

"Don't know what's keeping J.D.," she said after a while. "Go 'head and fix your plate."

"That's all right. I'll wait."

Finally, J.D. came to the table, pulling his chair out too rough, too fast, and sat down. He took a big spoon of squash from the pan and flicked his wrist hard above the plate. He handed the spoon to Baxter.

Cindy took two biscuits from the pan. She looked over at J.D., and he was looking at her.

"You starch every shirt I got?" he asked her.

"Just what I washed yesterday."

"I don't like that mess," he said.

"Hand me the salt, would you, J.D.?" Baxter said.

J.D. gave him the shaker and put pepper on his food.

The squash were right good, she thought, fresh and cooked tender. She had seasoned them with some fried meat grease she'd saved in a jar.

"Gonna have to check the 'bacca after dinner," J.D. said to Baxter with his mouth full.

"All right."

"Got to be sure the trenches is draining it all right. If that water stands there and it keeps this up, liable to get blue mold in it."

"Yeah," Baxter agreed. "I'll be checking on it soon as we eat."

"I'm going back out with you," J.D. said. "I was just saying it had to be done's all. Can't afford to lose the crop."

"Trenches ought to drain it off all right. It's them folks raising turkeys what better be worried."

"Yeah," J.D. said. "Drown 'em all if they ain't careful."

And J.D. was right. That's just the way baby turkeys were. Didn't have enough sense to get out of the shower of rain. And what was worse, they'd turn their heads right up to the sky when they were little like that and let it rain down their throats till they drowned.

"J.D.?" Cindy said.

"Yeah?"

"Better see 'bout a trench out there in the yard, too. Water's running clean through the outhouse."

"I'll look at it," he said.

After dinner J.D. and Baxter put their boots and hats back on and walked toward the tobacco fields. It was still raining right along, but it wasn't raining near as hard as it had been.

Cindy cleaned up from dinner and then took Callie to the bedroom. It wasn't time for the baby to be sleepy again, but she had to put her down so she could feed the chickens. She laid Callie in the cradle and got a sheet from the cedar chest at the foot of the bed. She spread the sheet over the top of the cradle and tied it at the corners, pulling it tight so it would not sag down and touch the baby. That way, she could go quick and feed the chickens and get up the eggs and not be scared to death that Callie was going to fall out on her head before she could get back.

J.D. was gonna have to get around to making her a crib. It was a shame she couldn't use the same one J.D. had used, but that was that. Nothing to be done about it but make a new crib. Mama Rose had saved J.D.'s cradle and crib, had them in a packhouse not far from the smokehouse. But a hand working for J.D.'s pa had tossed his cigarette over there near it on the ground one summer when it was hot as blazes and they hadn't had no rain for weeks. Mama Rose said when she looked, the whole thing was afire and the smoke was rolling. J.D.'s pa and the hand and little J.D. had come running up from the field when they saw it, but it wasn't no use. Burnt the whole thing to the ground.

Out in the chicken pen, she poured some corn onto the covered dry ground underneath the barrel. The three chickens inside pecked at it, taking a piece at a time into their beaks. She reached into the barrel under the chickens to be sure one hadn't laid an egg in there. Then she went to each nest looking for eggs, sprinkling some corn in each box where there was a chicken. J.D. wouldn't like it none if he knew she was feeding them that way, but what J.D. didn't know wouldn't hurt him. He'd tell her feeding them that way would make them lazy, make them just set right there in them nests all day long where they wouldn't get no fresh air and exercise. Then they'd stop laying. But she didn't feed them in the nests unless it was raining. To be sure feeding them like that was better than putting it on the ground where it would get soggy and they wouldn't eat it at all.

When she'd finished with the chickens, she poured two buckets of corn into the trough for the hogs. They grunted and came out from under their shelter to eat. They'd eat corn any way you gave it to them, wet or dry. They didn't even leave it there long enough for it to get soggy.

She liked the hogs. She knew most people didn't really care too much for them, just kept them around for meat, but they weren't so bad as folks made them out to be. They weren't all so dumb as folks thought, neither. She could tell them that. She wondered if they really liked being dirty like everybody thought they did. She didn't really think so. She figured they were just hot was all and that rolling 'round in the mud was about as good a way as they had for cooling off. Some days when it was real hot she'd tote buckets of water down there to the hog pen and pour it over them, and they seemed to like it just fine. Didn't roll in the mud, either, after she'd done that. They weren't nasty, just hot.

Inside the barn she fed the horses and the mule their omalene feed. She gave a little of it to Bessie, too, even though J.D. had said the cow didn't really need none of that. She acted like it was good, though, so Cindy let her have it. She gave her plenty of hay, too. She reached over the stall and rubbed the top of the cow's head. It was soft and dry, smooth as anything you ever felt if you rubbed it the right way. Bessie had not been outside in the rain. Cindy put her face up to the stall, and the cow touched her big, damp nose to Cindy's and breathed hot, moist air onto her face. Bessie turned back toward the feed box, sticking out her long, grayish tongue to get the sweet feed from the corners. She had touched Cindy with her tongue before, and it felt slightly rough against her skin. She watched the cow eat for awhile and then went on back to the house.

She untied the sheet from the corners of Callie's cradle and held her pressed into her side while she got a pair of J.D.'s overalls and two of his shirts from the bottom drawer of the dresser. She carried the baby into the parlor and set her in the middle of the braided rug. Then she sat in the rocker J.D. had made her for a wedding present. It was not as large as the rest of the chairs in there, made more to fit her size than a man's. She reached down beside the chair into her sewing box and got out a few buttons, comparing the size of each one to the size of the buttons on one of J.D.'s shirts till she found a match. She wondered how he managed to lose so many buttons even though she sewed them on good. Must catch them on stuff. But it did look like if he did, he'd know when he'd pulled one off and look for it. But no such luck. She was all the time telling him to pick up buttons at Parrish's, and that was in spite of her saving all the ones he had left on shirts when he wore them slam out and she had no choice but to throw them out.

It wasn't too often she threw a shirt out, or anything else for that matter. She'd patch and patch, patch over patches if she had to till the clothes would near about stand up on their own, and they'd keep on wearing the same stuff till there wasn't no fix to it. Had to.

As she sewed the button on with her needle and thread and made the rocking chair go with her foot, she thought of Mama at her sewing machine. Mama could make anything she set her mind to and you couldn't tell it didn't come straight from the store if you didn't look at the seams. Everybody swore up and down that the only difference in Mama's clothes and storebought was the fancy seams and topstitch they did at them factories. Mama would work that peddle with her foot and get that Singer going, and there wasn't a thing she couldn't do.

Mama'd made every dress Cindy ever wore from the time she was born till the day she got married and left there. Mama had spent many a hour making clothes for her, sewing every stitch of every piece with love. But sometimes Cindy had wished that just once she could have a dress from town, just go and get one right out of the window at Parrish's. There hadn't been no money for that, and she knew she better be thankful to the good Lord that she had never seen a time she didn't have something to wear, never seen a time when Mama didn't manage to get her a coat made somehow and Papa didn't manage to put shoes on her feet.

One day she'd get her a storebought dress, one day. Near about every one she'd ever worn had been made out of flour sacks, and the ones that weren't made out of them weren't nothing to write home about. Like the dress she got married in. Mama had told Papa they needed to go to Parrish's, needed to get some material to make her a new dress. There wasn't really no money for it, but Papa agreed she couldn't wear her same old stuff that day. He and Mama had paid for part of it and traded butter and eggs for part of it, but they got that material for her, and Mama made her a dress out of it. It wasn't none to her liking, even though she wouldn't've told them that for nothing. When they got there to buy it, she wanted some material off that bolt Mrs Parrish said they'd ordered from Philadelphia. It was pink with little blue flowers on it, pretty as anything you ever saw. But Mama said the wool would be more durable, and they'd take the brown. So there she was with a brown dress. Brown as in brown. She'd just as soon have anything besides brown.

She tied a knot on the back side of where she'd just sewn the button and cut the hanging strings. Then she folded the shirt and put it down on the side of the chair opposite her sewing box.

Callie whined a little, so Cindy gave her the string of spools to play with. The baby shook the spools, then chewed on one of them. Mama'd said she'd be this way, whining and wanting to chew on everything. She had in two of her teeth already, and Cindy could feel two more trying to come in.

She wondered where the time had gone since Callie was born. Already she was pulling herself up and cutting teeth. Wouldn't be notime before she was walking and talking. Cindy knew that's what babies were supposed to do, but sometimes she hated it that she had so much other stuff to do besides tending to Callie. She felt like Callie was going to be grown tomorrow and she'd wake up and realize she'd missed something while she was cooking and washing clothes, find out she didn't know that big girl at all that used to be her baby.

It was the same way with all mamas, she reckoned. Her mama said it was that way with her, couldn't believe it when she looked one day and her little Cindy was fifteen, near about sixteen, and getting married. Couldn't believe it at all.

She could remember Mama saying that same thing when her brother Jasper got married. Even though he was nineteen, Mama couldn't believe her firstborn wasn't a baby no more. Mama cried the day he got married, but then she wasn't all that sure that him being grown up was how come Mama was crying. A lot went on with that wedding, being as they had to have it fast and all. Him and his wife never had got on their feet. Still lived right there with Papa and Mama right now, them and little Tommy, in that small room Papa built onto the side of the house for them.

Jasper and his wife got married in Mama and Papa's house with just preacher Yates and the family there just like she and J.D. did, but their weddings weren't in no other ways alike. She never had understood that thing either. Mama and Papa had got her married off quick as they could, like their hats were on fire and their hind ends were catching, and she never had figured out why, unless they were scared of J.D. taking a liking to somebody else before time for a wedding. It wasn't her that had to be in no hurry. At least she hadn't had to get hitched before everybody in the county heard she was expecting.

She picked up J.D.'s other shirt and started fixing the tear on the back. He must have caught it on some wire. It would look bad where she sewed it back together, being as it was the material that was torn, not the seam, but at least there was some fix to it. Didn't matter to him none noway if it looked bad. Didn't matter to him not one bit how his clothes looked. Not that they could afford to do anything about it if it did.

She thought about how neat Sam had looked every time she'd seen him, always in pressed slacks and a crisp shirt. And of course his shoes didn't have not one scuff on them. She wondered if he'd still look the same as he had then. Probably would. She'd probably know him soon as she laid eyes on him. He'd know her, too. Only thing that had changed about her looks was that now she toted Callie around on one hip.

Cindy looked down at Callie playing on the floor.

"Want to go to town tomorrow?" she asked the baby. "Want to see something 'sides this same old house?"

Callie smiled, showing her teeth, like she knew what her mama had said. But Cindy knew she didn't. Callie was lucky, she thought. Wasn't big enough to recognize the sameness of the place, day in and day out. Still small enough to fill her days with a rag doll and a string of spools.

She would ask J.D. tonight about her going to town in the morning if it stopped raining. She'd fry some slices of ham and open up a jar of those garden peas with new potatoes he liked so good. She'd put up some of the peas each time she picked them and cooked a mess of 'em. She'd open them right up and feed J.D. a good supper, and then she'd ask him. Mama always said you wait till a man's got his belly full before you talk to him about anything. Said the key to a man's heart was through his stomach. She'd tell J.D. what they had to have and that she didn't mind a bit going instead of him.

It had been a long time since she went to town on Saturday morning, so many folks she hadn't seen in ages. She'd tell every one she saw to be sure to be at the church Sunday morning to share the morning with her and J.D. and Callie. And then she was sure she could find Sam, too, sure he'd be there trying to drum up business on the busiest day of the week in town.

She wanted to hear about all where he'd been again, and she'd be careful to take it all in when he told her, take in every word he said. And soon as her Callie was big enough to listen, she'd start telling her about them places even before she could read. She'd tell her and tell her as many times as she'd hear it that there was something out there besides mules and plows and Half Moon 'Cosin.

7

○ Ghosts ○

Cindy thumped the two big watermelons on the back porch. She'd asked Baxter to bring her up a couple as soon as he got there this morning while she was finishing breakfast and J.D. was getting dressed. Baxter swore J.D. had grown the biggest ones he'd ever seen, bigger than they had at the fair even. And she did have to say they were pretty as any she'd ever seen. J.D. had planted them down there by the creek where the dirt was sandy, same place his papa and grandpa had always planted. The sandier the dirt, the better the watermelons would grow, J.D. said.

The watermelons sounded all right when she thumped them, but she wanted to be sure before they cut them. She laid a piece of straw on top of the one closest to her and moved her fingers back away from it. Sure enough, the straw moved back and forth just a little on top of the watermelon. No question about it, it was ripe. She laid the straw on the other melon, and the straw moved on it, too. When she came back from town, she'd make them some sandwiches right quick for dinner. Then they'd cut big slices of watermelon and eat till they couldn't hold no more.

J.D. had said it would help out if she'd go to town. They were near about out of omalene and flour, too. It had stopped raining in the night. The fields would be muddy, but it had turned out to be a right pretty morning. J.D. and Baxter had just gone to the field. J.D. said they'd start back priming today as soon as they picked up whatever leaves the rain had beat off the stalks.

She went up to the bedroom and gave Callie a bath. Then she bathed herself and put on her best cotton dress. She pinned the little drawstring sack with the money J.D. had given her in it inside her slip to be sure she didn't lose it. He'd counted out what it would take to get the flour and the feed, and she had to be careful not to lose a cent of it.

J.D. always did business that way, counted out money for every item they had to buy one at a time. If he didn't have the cash for it, they didn't get it. Cash and carry or nothing. Of course not too many places were letting folks get much on the credit no more with times so bad, but even if they had been, he wouldn't've bought nothing that way. Just like her papa for the world when it came to money. Said they might live hand to mouth, but at least he wouldn't owe his soul.

When she was ready, she folded a sheet so that it would fit in her large wicker basket. She laid the sheet in the bottom for padding. Then she laid Callie in the basket and covered her with a thin, small blanket. She picked up the basket and went through the parlor and out the front of the house to where J.D. had left Nellie hitched to the wagon for her. She set the basket up on the seat and pushed it with one hand, sliding it across the bench. Pulling her skirt up a little with one hand and holding onto the handle on the side of the seat with the other, she climbed into the wagon and sat down, taking the reins in one hand and holding onto the basket with the other.

On the road she could hear the stickiness of the mud as the wheels rolled over it and pulled away. Better than it being dry and dusty as all getout, though. At least she and Callie wouldn't be covered in grit before they got there.

The sun was bright in her eyes when she started out of the trees that marked the boundary to the 'cosin. She squinted her eyes to the light and when she turned her head to the side to look down at the baby, she saw something out of the corner of her eye. Three backs in high-necked dresses, three bonnets to hold the hair, sitting across the back of the wagon, riding out of the 'cosin with her. She understood it, understood it good, taking a chance like that to see what was on the other side of those trees. So she kept on going, kept on driving that wagon right on past those trees to where the road was straight, not curved into the stiffness of the new moon.

Maybe, just maybe, she wasn't so different as she had thought from all the other women of the 'cosin. Just because a woman was a good wife and mother and knew her place all the days of her life, didn't mean that she was happy there, didn't mean she never wondered sometimes about what might be outside her own walls. Maybe it had been the same for all of them. And maybe they were all like her, like an animal in a fence that knows the grass is greener on the other side of those rails but is afraid it's not strong enough to break out and way too scared to eat a thing besides just what's handed to it.

She looked back at the road to be sure she was holding the reins so the horse would go straight. Then she looked out across the fields that stretched on and on till the sky grew out of them.

After a ways she passed the lane leading up to the Partins' place. She could make out the figure of a woman on the porch, and she could see Clara Lou waving to her as she went by. She raised up her arm from the basket and waved back.

Still, she kept on going, going on quick as she could without putting a strain on Nellie. She braced herself, stiffened her back as the big wheels rolled over the bumps and fell into the holes. Still, she didn't slow down, but held on even tighter, and she knew without looking that they held on, too. That was the way they all had lived, she supposed, the way she was living now, holding on tight to get up the hills, holding on tight to pull up from the valleys. And still they kept on going.

When she was sure she was where no one would hear, she began to sing at the top of her voice, singing to the baby and the weeds and the rabbit at the side the road that did not run from the horse and the noise. And the words came out and out and out, words she had never used together before to a melody she did not know. But the words came out, and they were beautiful. The women of the 'cosin sang with her.

So on they went, holding on and singing like younguns on a hayride in the fall. She couldn't remember when she'd felt this good, when she'd felt anything but tired and dead on her feet. Couldn't remember when she'd breathed this deep, or when the air had been so fresh.

And on they went till she could see the town up ahead and stopped her singing and turned around to look at the women. She drove on into town, past the church and school, with not one soul in the wagon besides her and Callie. And she understood it, understood it good, wanting to get out of that 'cosin and not being able to let it show.

She pulled on the reins to stop Nellie in front of the general store. Inside, the Parrishes were mighty tickled to see her. Hadn't seen her in a blue moon, they said.

"Just as purty as any youngun I ever saw," Mrs Parrish said of Callie. Said she was sorry she never had got out there to see them after the baby was born, but things had been so busy with her helping Mr P. full time in the store now and all. Said Mr P. was counting on her now. Couldn't afford to pay as much help as he used to. Had to let Buck Connell go, on account of it.

But she knew how come Mrs Parrish hadn't come out there. She wasn't about to go riding into them haunted woods of the 'cosin by herself. Hadn't nobody been there to see her at all except her own folks and Janie, and nobody was going to come either.

She said her goodbyes and started out of the store, surprised that it wasn't full of folks on Saturday morning.

Maybe things had got worse than she knew over those months she hadn't come to town. Shorty Parrish toted the heavy sacks out to the wagon for her and put them on the back. Mrs Parrish said Shorty had to do all the lifting since Mr P. hurt his back. Good thing they had him around there, she said.

"Push them sacks up a little further in the wagon, would you, Shorty?" Cindy said.

"Yes'm."

Shorty pushed the big bags toward the back of the seat. His arms weren't long, but big around, strong.

"You 'specting to load something else on the back, are you?"

"Naw, just want to be sure the sacks don't fall off,'s'all. Road out there's mighty bumpy."

Shorty Parrish shook his head and went back in the store. She hated to make up excuses like that, but there wasn't any way she was going to tell him how come she needed the back of that wagon empty. Who was going to believe she had folks riding back to the 'cosin with her? Everybody 'round there for miles knew you could count the folks on your two hands who would go near that place.

She had thought she might see Sam hanging 'round the store, that if he wasn't selling his shoes to Mr Parrish, to be sure he'd be out in front trying to sell to whoever come up. But she didn't see hide nor hair of him, so she decided to leave the wagon right there a minute and go across the street to visit with Miss Lyda.

"Cindy, I don't know when in the cat hair I've seen you, girl," Miss Lyda said.

Cindy looked at the old woman, taking in how much Miss Lyda had aged since she last saw her. Her hair wasn't even gray no more. It was slam white.

"Come on to the back with me, will you? Got my irons on the stove heating."

"Can't stay but a minute," Cindy said. "Got to get back to the house and fix some dinner for J.D. and Baxter."

"He a hard worker?" Miss Lyda lifted the first black iron from the stove by its wood-covered handle.

"Yeah, works real good. Does anything you ask him to and don't complain 'bout a thing."

"Seems to me to be a right nice boy, what I see of him 'round here at night. It's a shame 'bout his daddy losing their farm, ain't it?"

"Sure is," Cindy said.

Miss Lyda went on ironing and talking about how fine a fellow Baxter was till the iron she was using cooled off too much. Then she set that iron back on the stove and picked up the other one with a rag. It didn't have a wood handle to protect her hand from the heat.

"I iron this boy's shirts till my arm near 'bout falls off. Got to have 'em pressed just so."

She turned the shirt around on the ironing board to iron up next to the collar.

"Pays me extra for it though."

"Heard you've got a visitor," Cindy said.

"Yeah, that's whose shirts these are. Sells shoes."

"That's what Baxter was telling us," Cindy said.

"I told him not to expect to do a whole lot of business 'round here this year, but he seems to want to stay on a while. All right with me long as he's paying regular."

"Wonder if he's sold a single pair," Cindy said.

"Just a couple's what he told me. Gone out there to Nichols' store trying to sell today."

She hadn't thought of him being at Nichols', that little hole-in-the-wall country store out there at the crossroads between town and Buddy Albritton's place. Wasn't much that went on out that way except for the men that lived 'round there playing cards in the store at night and folks stopping by to see if Joe Nichols would sell them some moonshine out from under the counter. Papa said he had the biggest still in the county in them woods out there behind his house.

Everybody 'round there said that store was what did Buddy's wife Gertie in. They'd found her in the pond way at the back of Buddy's land. He said she must've been picking the flowers and slipped, but everybody knew it wasn't no such a thing. They'd bet their farms she'd just walked right off in the water. All the men 'round there who helped Buddy look for her said there wasn't a mark around that pond nowhere where she might have slipped in. Just couldn't take the drinking and the gambling no more. Buddy'd lost everything he had except the farm and the shirt on his back betting every stranger that come through town that he could make a better hand of cards than they could. Some folks said you could still walk back there by that pond late of an evening and hear a woman crying.

"Well, I wish him luck out there," Cindy said.

"Yeah, me too."

She and Miss Lyda went on talking till Cindy told her she really had to get on back and fix dinner. Outside, she crossed back over to Parrish's and set Callie up on the wagon seat. Before she could get in and drive off, here come Pansie from over at the bank toward the store.

She never had liked that Pansie Parker. Never had liked her one bit. Back when Cindy was in school, Pansie always let the farmers' younguns know she was better than them 'cause her daddy worked in the bank. One time her daddy'd whipped her good, give her a good thrashing right there in front of all of them at school because he found out Pansie'd told little Johnny Mason she could get her daddy to take their farm when his pa was down sick.

She'd made little Johnny cry something awful. Didn't nobody like that Pansie Parker. Always thought she was pretty as ever walked. Ugly as homemade soap was more like it. Had them big moles all on her face, and had the nerve to call them marks of beauty. Pretty only to a lying mirror.

"Morning, Cindy," Pansie said. She passed behind the wagon to go into the store. "Nice dress. You must like them flour sacks."

Cindy could hear the bell at the top of the door ringing as the door closed behind her.

She pulled the reins so that Nellie turned the wagon around, and she headed out of town the same way she'd come in. She passed the schoolhouse and felt right sorry for herself, sorry she had to leave there, sorry that on her first trip to town in so long she hadn't been able to see Janie. Janie had gone off for two weeks to that summer retreat for teachers two counties over. Left a couple of days before.

She'd bet it was pretty there. Janie said it was a big white house, bigger than any rooming house she'd ever seen, just a ways from the bank of the Neuse River. Weeping willows hung down everywhere you looked, Janie said. Maybe Janie would send her a letter from there to tell her more about it. If she did, she'd be back by the time Cindy got it. It wasn't so easy getting mail there in the 'cosin. Old

Elias Jeb Trenton ran their route, but he said he'd give up his job before he went down in that 'cosin by himself. Said he'd heard the first and only mailman to go in there after J.D.'s great-grandfather moved in there never come out. Elias Jeb swore up and down something got him, the horse, and all. She never had believed a word of it, but that didn't make no difference to Elias Jeb. Wasn't nothing you could've said to him that would have made a difference. Hadn't been no mail in the 'cosin in so many years that J.D. finally took the mailbox up and moved it down there beside the Partins'. Abe had said it was all right to put it there. Might as well put it there. Elias Jeb had been leaving their mail down there at the Partins' ever since she'd come there, being as it was the last farm before the 'cosin. Still, they had to wait for the mail. J.D. was funny about it. Wanted to get it himself. Didn't want her to go get it. Didn't want Baxter to pick it up and bring it of a morning. But then, J.D. was doing good if he remembered to go down there and get it one time a week. Still, she hoped Janie would send a letter and tell her all about who she'd met there and what counties they taught in and how long those willows hung down.

When she got out of town, she didn't go straight on down Long Pine road. Instead, she took the fork that would take her by the crossroads. She'd hurry.

She'd cut back across to Long Pine from there and get on home and fix dinner. But first she'd see if Sam was still out there at Nichols'. It wasn't too far out of the way. She'd just ride by there and see if he was out front and might see her and wave for her to stop.

J.D. would never get over it if he knew she'd come by this way looking for a shoe salesman she could have run off with. He'd never believe she wasn't trying to get up a case with him, wasn't making plans to leave. She drove on fast as she could go, hoping she wouldn't meet nobody along the road that would see J.D. and tell him they'd seen her. Maybe she shouldn't have come this way.

But even if J.D. found out, it would be worth her coming down here if she could talk to Sam and take in all he had to say. She could go through a lot, live through many a day of J.D. being mad as a wet setting hen if she had those places Sam had seen in her head. And she'd save every word he said for Callie to hear. She'd wrap each detail in paper and pack 'em all away in the boxes in her mind for her baby.

And when Callie was big enough to understand, she'd unpack those boxes for her one at a time and show her all the treasures inside. She'd tell her about every place she'd heard of, make her see how each one shined in its own way like a jewel. Callie would be able to do two things Cindy never had been able to do. One day Callie would wear a jewel, and she'd get to pick which one she wore.

Cindy could see the country store in the distance. Sure enough, she could make out the shape of a car. She turned around and looked down in the back of the wagon, looked at the sack of flour and omalene feed. She held on tight to the basket so it wouldn't fall when she stopped the wagon.

Sam was sitting up under the shelter in front of the store in a cane-bottomed chair. The back of the chair rested up against the front of the building, the front legs up off the ground.

Sam opened his eyes when he heard the wagon stop. He smiled when he saw it was her, but he didn't look at her much. Kept his eyes on her basket, waiting to see what it was she had.

She took the basket down and walked 'round in front of the horse to where he was.

"Hello there, Sam Barker," she said to him.

He widened his smile into a grin, but he kept on looking at her. He recognized her. That was for sure. But for a second she thought he must not be able to think of her name. That was all right, though. As many people as a man like him saw in a day, how could anybody expect him to remember all them names?

His hair was shining on one side where the sun was coming up under the shelter and hitting it. It looked sort of like embers do when a fire is dying down but there's still a little life in it, not all cold, gray ashes.

"Remember me? Cindy?"

"Clear as a bell," he said. "Aint never forgot that dinner you fixed me that day. Best sandwiches I ever had in my life."

"So how've you been?"

"Oh, all right, I reckon. 'Bout the same. Still selling shoes. How you doing?"

"Fair, I reckon," she said. "Got married since I saw you last. This here's my baby, Callie."

She held the oval basket down so he could see.

He reached into the basket and touched Callie's face with one finger. His hands were clean, smooth. Had his fingernails trimmed up just so. Wasn't a one of them broke off ragged like he'd been doing no work.

"Just as purty as her mama," Sam said.

Joe Nichols pushed open the screen door, the spring creaking, and came out of the store. He let the door slam shut behind him. In his hand he had a Co-cola. He took a sip from the small, light green bottle and belched. She could see it wasn't the first thing he'd had to drink this morning.

"Thought I heard somebody," he said, his red, watery eyes fixed on her.

"Morning, Joe," she said.

"Help you with something?"

Not if it was the last help she'd ever get. Old drunk, nasty thing. Nasty as a buzzard. Had on one of them aprons that tied behind his neck and at the small of his back. Supposed to be white. Had dried up bits of cheese and what she reckoned was sausage on it where he must've been grinding the day before. Wasn't a thing he had that she would have bought. Not even if it was the last store on the face of the earth.

"No, thanks," she said. "Stopped to see 'bout some shoes, but I reckon I'd best be getting on back home. J.D.'s gonna be waiting on his dinner as it is."

Sam looked at her, looked at her close like he was trying to see if she'd sewn one of the seams crooked on her dress.

"I'll stop by one day and show you some things, then," he said. "How you say you get there?"

She pointed which way to go from the crossroads.

"Take that on out till it dead ends. Turn right. That's Long Pine Road. Just stay on it till you get into a 'cosin. The only house in there'll be us."

"Easy enough," he said.

He brushed his hair back away from his face with one hand. A gold ring with a big red stone glittered in the sun. You sure could tell he wasn't used to working in no fields. All that hair falling in his eyes would drive him crazy if he did. All the men around there kept theirs cropped off short all the time. Didn't let it get more than half way down above their eyebrows.

"Don't know if I'd go in there if I was you," Joe said, belching again.

Cindy went back to the wagon, set the baby up there, and then got in herself.

"Sure there ain't something I can sell you?"

"Not today, Joe," she said.

She slapped the reins lightly against the horse, not hard like J.D. did it, to make her go.

"Be seeing you," Sam said. He leaned up against the wall again and closed his eyes.

Joe Nichols didn't say another word. Just turned around and went back in his store, letting the screen door slam behind him like he was mad. Nasty buzzard.

She headed on down the road the way she'd just shown Sam. She didn't look back to see if he was watching her. Just told herself he'd kept his eyes closed like they were when she left. She never had been able to stand it when somebody was staring at her. Tore her nerves all to pieces. Lot of times she didn't even have to look to see when somebody was watching her. She could feel, feel it right to the bone, when somebody was looking at her. That's the way that stupid Pansie Parker used to do her. Pansie could stare a hole through anybody, looking them over from head to toe and then toe to head to see what they were wearing and if one hair was out of place. She was glad when she rounded a curve and was sure she was out of sight of the store.

She wondered when Sam would come. He hadn't said, just said he'd come. Now all she could do was hope he'd come when J.D. was out in the field. Heaven have mercy on her if Sam came there with J.D. at the house. He'd be mad as fire, and she wouldn't be able to ask Sam a thing.

She thought about Sam sitting up under the shelter at the store. Except for his clothes, he reminded her of her Uncle Willard sitting under there with his chair leaned back. She didn't remember ever seeing Uncle Willard sit any other way. Of course, she never had been around him all that much, and it had been more than six years since the last time she saw him. Been that long since any of them had seen him.

Uncle Willard never had been one for funning. Papa and Uncle Burt ought to have known better than to play that trick on him at the reunion. Ought to have known he'd get fighting mad about it. But they'd done it, and that was that.

He'd always been the lazy one in the bunch, they said. When they were younguns, he'd let their pa near about beat him to death rather than pick a sack of cotton. Sometimes he'd be asleep at the end of the field, leaned up against a tree. All the rest of the younguns would put a little of their cotton in his sack so that Papa'd think he'd been working and wouldn't beat him so bad. They were scared that one of those days Papa was gonna beat him to death. But Willard wouldn't work for nothing. They'd tell him and tell him, "Pa's gonna beat the daylights outta you," but it didn't make him no nevermind. He was just that stubborn, just that john-browned lazy.

And when he come there for that last reunion, he still hadn't changed one bit. Wouldn't even get up to pitch horseshoes with them. Just sat right there on the porch leaned back in a chair.

So Papa and Uncle Burt had waited till he went to sleep. They knew it wouldn't be long. He had always been one to fall asleep as soon as he got his belly full. And as soon as he did, they eased right out there to the chicken yard and scooped them up a big pile. Wasn't nothing that smelled no worse than fresh chicken do, and they put some right in the palm of his hand. Then Uncle Burt had took him a feather and rubbed under Uncle Willard's nose, tickled it under there to make him think it was a fly. When Uncle Willard went to slap that fly, he got that stinking chicken do all in his face, and he jumped up cussing and hotter than a forty-five.

Never had been back to see Papa or Uncle Burt even though they'd told him they were just funning with him. And that's just who Sam looked like sitting there. Only he had on his same pressed clothes instead of overalls and brogan shoes, and to be sure he could take a joke better than Uncle Willard. Anybody could take a joke better than him.

At the end of the road, she made her turn back onto Long Pine and safety. Nobody had seen her but Joe Nichols, and she wasn't worried about him none. He stayed so drunk he didn't know from one day to the next who'd even been in the store.

She headed on toward the 'cosin. She had to get on back, had to fix some dinner, but she hated to go back. The 'cosin was like a pocket on J.D.'s overalls, deep and secret. Couldn't see out of it no matter how hard you tried once you were inside.

Before she got to the Partins' place she stopped the wagon at the side of the road. She got off and picked some of the fern that grew wild among the daisies by the ditchbank. When things started drying out in the fall, she'd come back and pick some cattails from out of the ditch. She always thought they were pretty to put on the porch. Things didn't grow wild like that in the 'cosin. Not flowers anyway. Just grass and trees and whatever J.D. planted. Nothing with color, nothing happy, not even down by the creek.

When she turned around to get back in the wagon, she was almost blinded by the sun, moving ever higher overhead. She shielded her eyes with her hand. Three old-timey dresses with bonnets to match, three pairs of shoes, thin heeled and laced high. They were picking daisies. She understood it, understood it good, that longing to take pieces of what was outside back to the 'cosin. She climbed back up to the seat and waited for them.

Then on they went back toward the 'cosin, back where they would just as soon not go. Like a watch on a chain, they could go only so far, only stay out so long before they went back in the pocket.

When she started into the trees, she could hear a dull hum, steady and sad. It was even and unending, reminded her of the bees around the hive Papa had back in the woods. Only she and J.D. didn't have no bees. No flowers, no bees. Got all their honey from her papa. But as she went back into the 'cosin, she could hear the humming, low and sad.

She pulled the wagon up behind the house and stopped it there. J.D. and Baxter would be up soon. She'd asked them to get the heavy sacks out for her and put Nellie up.

On the back of the wagon, she found three bunches of daisies laid neat in a row. But the ones who picked them had gone on back to wherever it was they stayed, leaving her those flowers, roots and all, perfect as if they had dug them up with little spades. She carried the daisies up on the porch and put them on the shelf not far from the pump. She pumped some water into a small pail, dipped it up in her cupped hand and sprinkled the water over the roots so they wouldn't dry out before she could plant them. They meant for her to plant them.

She carried Callie and the ferns into the house. She put the ferns in a mason jar with water and set it in the middle of the table.

At the counter she sliced the ends off cucumbers and ran the knife blade just under the skin to peel them. She sliced them thin and put the cucumbers between bread with salt and pepper and a little of the mayonnaise she kept in the icebox. She liked cucumbers right good, but she sure did hate to pick them. Had all them little prickly things on them, made her hands itch for two solid hours after she picked them.

Out the window she could see J.D. and Baxter coming to the house. She set the sandwiches on plates, put them on the table and then put two eggs in a small pot to boil. That's what she'd feed Callie. The baby wasn't going to eat no cucumbers.

She went to the back door and called to them.

"Tend to that for me, will you?"

"Sure thing," Baxter said.

J.D. lifted the sack of flour off the wagon and carried it inside to the pantry. Baxter took the horse, wagon, and feed to the barn.

"Rain beat off much 'bacca?" she asked J.D. when he came out of the pantry.

"Not bad as I 'spected. Picked it all up."

"Good." She set glasses on the table and poured water from a heavy pitcher.

Good thing they'd been able to save what was on the ground. It might not be much, but every leaf counted. Every leaf added its weight to the bundles of cured tobacco J.D. would carry wrapped in burlap sheets to the warehouse in a few more weeks.

She wondered what it would bring this year. Not as much as last year, that was for sure.

She had always loved it when the warehouse opened. When she was a youngun, Papa let her go with him a few times. She could still remember how good it smelled in there, like Papa's barn at home, only ten times as sweet and strong. She tried to listen to what was going on, but that man selling it just talked way too fast, and she never had been able to keep up.

But then she was glad, too, when all the tobacco was sold for the year, and it was time for the fair. She loved the fair like a hog loves slops. It was the best thing that happened in them parts all year. Everybody went to it before they started picking their corn.

When Baxter came in, they sat down to eat. She left Callie on the floor, hoping she'd play and not get to crying before the eggs got done.

J.D. and Baxter talked about the rain and the mud and how good it was for the corn. She kept an eye on the pot, water flying out of it once in a while and sizzling away on the stove. When the eggs were done, she took the pot from the stove and carried it out to the pump where she added cold water till the pot ran over. She peeled the eggs, cracking the big ends first like Mama always told her to do so the whites wouldn't tear up so bad. She let the pieces of the shells drop over the rail to the ground.

Inside, she mashed the eggs and fed them to the baby. When they finished eating, she got one of the watermelons from the porch, and J.D. sliced it on the table. They ate half of it, the other half still sitting in a puddle of juice on the table. This afternoon, she was going to make rind preserves.

Rind preserves always reminded her of that joke her Papa told over and over to anybody what would listen. It was his favorite. She didn't really know why. These two little boys were setting in the dirt. One was eating a slice of watermelon. The other little boy didn't have none, so he told the first little boy, "Hey, save me the rind when you get through." And the first little boy said, "There ain't gonna be no rind."

As soon as J.D. and Baxter went back to the field, she went outside to plant the daisies. She'd wipe the table and clean the kitchen when she made preserves, after she planted the flowers and tended to the animals.

She set Callie on a quilt out in the front yard and dug little holes all around the porch. She set one plant in each hole, careful to cover the roots good to hold the daisies there, but not mashing down so hard she broke the roots. Wouldn't nothing survive long with no roots. Then she watered them all from the pail she'd toted 'round there to the front.

It was beautiful around the porch when she got through. Spots of white with bright yellow centers against the darkness of the space under the house, against the grayness of the stones in the pillars the house set up on.

She looked off down the road at nothing and then back at the flowers. She could hear the whole 'cosin breathing in deep, drawing long, wonderful breaths to smell the daisies.

She felt good, like she was breathing for the first time since she'd come there.

8

○ The Visit ○

Cindy watered the daisies 'round the porch, holding the pail close to the ground so the water wouldn't break the small stems. She poured the water next to the base of each plant.

J.D. hadn't even noticed that she'd put flowers 'round the porch. Come to think of it, he hadn't been 'round the front of the house at all since she planted them, and that had been right many days. He and Baxter were down at the barn sheeting tobacco. That's all he'd talked about for days was getting his tobacco to town and the warehouse opening.

She moved on from plant to plant, watering each one like she'd seen her mama water hills of squash in the garden when it was dry. She was just about through when she heard the car coming.

Sam pulled the car up close to the porch.

"Just like you said. Only house in the 'cosin," he said as he got out of the car.

"Yeah, that's us," she said. She set the pail down and walked over near his car. "Glad you come. Have a seat here on the porch."

The sun reflected off his big gold belt buckle and shined in her eyes.

"You wanting to look at some shoes?"

"Well, I was kinda wanting to talk to you," she said.

"All right. We'll talk and then look at some shoes."

He followed her up on the porch and sat down in a rocker.

"Can I get you something to drink?"

"Naw, I'm fine right now. Thank you, though."

"All right," she said. "Let me see 'bout my baby. She's been sleeping in the house. Be right back."

"Take your time. Take your time."

She went in the house and came back with the baby. She sat in the swing and let the baby sit up on her lap.

"She's a cutie all right," Sam said.

"Thank you," Cindy said. "I think so myself, but then every mama thinks her baby's the purtiest one there ever was, I reckon."

"Bet she's a real papa's girl."

Cindy looked away from him. She looked at the side of his car, dark and shiny with some mud splattered up from the wheels.

"So what'd you want to talk about?" he asked her. He pushed the hair away from his eyes.

"I want you to tell me 'bout your life," she said.

"My life? Ain't much to tell. I sell shoes."

"No, that ain't what I mean. You said you been a lot of places, and I want to hear 'bout 'em all."

"Yeah, I do get around, I reckon," he said.

"See, I ain't never been nowhere," she said, "and I want to hear 'bout where you've been."

"Ain't much to tell. Places is places, some bigger, some smaller, but still just places."

She got up from the swing and walked to the edge of the porch. She looked at his car, heard the little popping sounds of the motor cooling off kind of like her stove did if she let it go out. She felt like she could just run down those steps and jump in that car and go. She turned back around to face Sam, leaning her back up against one of the columns that ran from the floor to the roof on the porch, Callie in her arms.

Places weren't all the same, and she knew it. Every place was different in its own way, different from this 'cosin where she was fenced in.

"You drive this car all the way from Memphis?" she asked him.

"Yeah, been a long way with that car. Hoping to get something else soon as things get better, though."

"You gonna get rid of your car?"

"Naw, just trade it in for something better, another kind."

"Oh." She didn't know there was another kind. A car was a car so far as she knew.

"See, this here's a Ford, a Model A roadster they call it. Twenty-nine model. I'm gonna get me a Packard DeLuxe Eight 745. Long and looks good. Comes where you can let the top to it down and ride."

She'd never seen such a thing, and she wondered what in the world he'd want it for. Might as well ride in a wagon like she and J.D. did if you weren't gonna have no roof over your head. Least it'd get you around fast, she reckoned.

"You been back home lately?"

"Not in a while," he said. "Think I might head back for a spell after the fair. Gonna set up a booth there and sell. Then I'll go home."

Cindy took the few steps back over to the swing and sat down. She looked at him, looked at how his hands were not rough, how his clothes were clean. Didn't seem to have a care in the world besides driving 'round asking folks if they were needing some shoes. The light breeze bent the daisy stems a little. She squinted her eyes, and it seemed like the daisies were smiling at her.

"Some days I wish I'd gone with you," she said.

He looked like she'd thrown a bucket of cold water on him. He stared at her, his mouth slightly open as if he wanted to say something and couldn't find a single word.

"J.D.'d want to skin me alive if he heard me say it," she said, "but some days I think I'd be better off if I'd jumped in that car and gone with you and never come back."

"Ain't no place for a woman on the road," he said finally.

"But you said—"

"I know it, but I didn't think you was taking me serious. I was just kidding 'round with you was all."

She felt just like she was sitting there naked in front of him, hurt that he hadn't meant it and embarrassed as all get-out that he knew she'd believed him. When was she ever going to learn that you just can't trust a man?

She sat there looking at a knothole in one of the boards on the floor of the porch. If it was big enough, she'd crawl right in it and hide. She could feel him looking at her, and she hoped her face wasn't red.

"Don't feel bad about it," he said after a while. "'Course you thought I was serious. Shouldn't've said it if I didn't mean it."

"No, you shouldn't've," she said, looking up at him.

"Sorry."

She set Callie down on the porch in front of her and looked away to the edge of the 'cosin. Neither one said a word for a long time.

All them days she'd spent thinking about how things might have been, and he hadn't meant a word of it. She felt hot from the inside out like she was about to faint. He hadn't meant not nary a word of it.

"Your husband 'round?" he asked her finally.

"Yeah, him and a hand's down there finishing sheeting 'bacca. Reckon I best be fixing their dinner."

She picked up Callie and started in the door, hoping he'd just leave. But he followed her on in the house and all the way back to the kitchen.

"Mind if I join you?" he asked her after he sat down at the table.

"Might as well. Already in here," she said.

She turned around to work at the counter, leaving him nothing to look at but her back. He sat there while she sliced tomatoes and heated corn on the stove.

"You fixing 'mater sandwiches?" he asked her after a while.

"You want one?"

"Wouldn't mind it."

She took another ripe tomato from the window sill and began slicing it. She could feel he was still watching her close.

"Know what else I wouldn't mind?" he said.

She turned around and faced him. What else wouldn't he mind? She'd just love to know. Come there and tell her he didn't really never plan on taking her with him, invite himself to dinner. Why not find out just what else it was he wanted?

He reached out and took hold of her arm about halfway between her hand and her elbow and tried to pull her to him like he wanted her to sit in his lap. But she pulled away from him.

"Wouldn't mind it at all if you was to go with me when I leave."

She felt like somebody'd hit her with a board. Couldn't believe he just said that to her. She turned away from him and leaned up against the counter, looking at the cobweb in the corner of the window outside. She didn't say a thing, just looked and looked at the pattern of the little strings in the web and at the fly trying to get out of it. Why didn't it just fly away? Looked like its wings were strong enough to get away from whatever hold the web had on its little legs.

"I ain't kidding this time, Cindy," he said. "I ain't playing."

"I'm married," she said, still looking at the fly. "That's how come you asked me now, 'cause you know I can't go."

"You can go," he said.

"And leave Callie?"

She moved over to the stove and stirred the corn to keep it from sticking.

"We'll take the baby with us."

She kept on stirring the corn, scraping her spoon against the bottom of the frying pan like Mama had always told her to. Weren't many things that tasted worse than scorched corn, and weren't nothing worse to wash than food burnt onto the bottom of a frying pan.

"You hear me? I said the baby can go, too."

"I heard you. But you said yourself the road ain't nowhere for a woman. So what kind of place is it for a baby?"

"She'll be all right. I promise. Y'all can go with me when I leave, and we'll go to Memphis and stay with Mammy till I can find us a place."

She set the corn in the middle of the table. Callie crawled out from underneath it and hit Cindy's foot.

"Girl, you better watch out 'fore I drop this hot corn on you."

Callie crawled right on by her, not paying her any mind at all. Good thing she wasn't big enough to talk and tell J.D. what her and Sam had been talking about. Younguns have a way of doing that, telling the very thing you don't want nobody else to know. Her folks had always said so. Said don't never do nothing in front of a youngun you don't want them to do and don't never say nothing you don't want one to tell 'cause they'll go straight and do it. Mama said a youngun was a mirror of its folks.

She looked at Callie and realized that she wouldn't remember this at all. Wouldn't remember Sam ever coming there to see her. Wouldn't remember J.D. or this house or this 'cosin if her mother was to run off with this man right now.

She wondered if anybody'd really ever done that, run off with somebody else when their younguns were too little to remember a thing about it. The younguns would just always think that was their daddy, she reckoned. What kind of daddy would Sam make? She wondered. Would he be sorry later on about having another mouth to feed? Would he want boys and nothing else?

"Reckon I'd better be getting out of here before your husband comes in for dinner. Don't need to see me here if we're gonna take off."

He stood up and pushed his chair under the table.

"I didn't say I was going," she said.

"Didn't say you weren't, neither."

"I don't know. How can I just pick up and go like that? Just don't seem right."

"Up to you," he said, "but you've got to make up your mind."

"Might as well take your sandwich with you," she said, handing it to him.

"Thank you. Y'all going to the fair, are you?"

"Yeah."

"If you're going, you be ready when you go to the fair. Pack you and the baby just what you can get by with, and put your case down there in the woods at the edge of the 'cosin."

She followed him to the front door and watched him walk to his car.

"Right down there in the woods," he said pointing. "We'll leave from the fair. Just meet me at my booth."

She watched him drive away, a little dust trailing out behind him where the dirt had dried out. When the car went through the trees and out of sight, she leaned back against the door frame. She felt limp as a dishrag.

Did he mean it? No. He hadn't meant it before, had he? Of course he didn't mean it. He knew she couldn't go. Knew she couldn't take no baby on the road like that.

Did he mean it? Maybe he did. Said he shouldn't say things he didn't mean. Of course he meant it. She could pack up and go, just grab up Callie and go.

What was she going to do? She was going to finish putting dinner on the table before J.D. found out. That's what she was going to do.

She hoped J.D. and Baxter wouldn't stay up long for dinner, hoped J.D. would go on back down to the barn so she could think. She couldn't think clear with him in there, specially not now. She felt like he'd just look right through her into her head and know what was going on. She needed to think by herself. Seemed like J.D. was always in a hurry to get to work when she wanted him to talk to her and always slow as Christmas when she wanted him to go on and leave her alone. Maybe today would be different with him wanting to get the crop to town and all. She hoped.

For goodness sake, she couldn't let him see through her now, couldn't let him see what kind of girl he was really married to, her there in his house with his baby thinking about running off with another man. How had it come to this? If anybody'd ever told her she'd be married to one man and thinking like this about another one, she would never have believed them. Of course she never would have believed she'd ever get married or live here. How had it come to this? Same old answer. Papa'd thought it was best. But it wasn't what was best for her. She'd known it then, and she knew it now. Wasn't what was best for her at all.

What was she going to do? She was going to put those tomato sandwiches on the table and bowls for the corn.

When J.D. and Baxter came in for dinner, they were full of talk about how they'd finish up right after dinner and start hauling the tobacco to town two wagon loads at a time. Baxter had asked Miss Lyda about using her wagon, and she had said it was all right. So him and J.D. would get it all to the warehouse two times as fast. They were happy as jaybirds and didn't pay her much mind at all. She was glad.

She fed Callie from her bowl of corn and ate a little of it herself, but not much. She didn't even bother with a sandwich. How could she eat with her nerves all tore up like this? What if J.D. found out? Beyond the shadow of a doubt, he'd string her up a tree. Heaven help her. He'd string her up a tree.

She felt like she'd been holding her breath all through dinner and that she finally let it out when J.D. and Baxter went back to the barn. She carried Callie to the bedroom and put her in the cradle. The baby felt too heavy to her, but she knew it was just her feeling weak and not really the baby at all. Wasn't no way Callie could've grown that much since this morning.

She pulled her case out from under the bed and dusted it off with a rag. Granda gave her that case, but she didn't really know why. It wasn't like she had nowhere to go. She'd only used it two times since the day she got it. One time to go spend the night at Granda's and then when she'd come here with J.D. the day she got married. She opened it up on the bed and sat down beside it. She picked up the little sachet Granda had put inside and held it by one corner, the lemon scent still there, not faded away one bit. It was an orangey-red, about the color of a red dog sun. She thought about the red dog sun. Papa always said if the sky looked that way when the sun was going down, all red and streaked on the horizon, the next day would be clear and cold. That was just the way she felt right now, like she was breathing in cold air, scared to breathe too deep or her insides might freeze. She just felt funny all over, tight and stiff like she'd been hanging out clothes in the dead of winter. Just felt funny all over.

What would Granda think if she knew what Cindy was thinking about doing with this case she gave her? Probably be enough to make her heart cut up something awful. Same with Mama and Papa. They would never have got over it if she'd run off with Sam before she was married, and for sure they'd never live it down if she was to do it now.

How had it come to this, her sitting here thinking this way? Just where had she crossed the line? She didn't know. All she knew was that when she came here, she thought she'd be here for the rest of her life because it was what she was supposed to do. Now here she was thinking about running off and didn't even know when it was that she decided enough was enough. Had it been the day Callie was born? Was it Callie she was really trying to get out of the 'cosin, or was she just being selfish, trying to get out because she wanted out? Had she gone over the line the day she went to town by herself? Or had she crossed it today? She didn't know. She didn't know anything at all. She felt like she was standing in the middle of the creek after a heavy rain and the water was about to carry her away, like she could see the bank on both sides but couldn't tell which one to go to.

She folded some clothes for her and the baby, a blanket, things J.D. would never miss, and put them in her case. She closed it and slid it back up under the bed. When J.D. went to town, she would tote it down there and set it in the woods at the edge of the 'cosin. How had it ever come to this?

9

○ At the Fair ○

Cindy set a basket on the table and laid a clean dishrag in the bottom of it. From a shelf in the pantry she got a jar of her watermelon rind preserves. Then she put in half a dozen of the best squash that she'd washed out at the pump and let dry in the sun. Maybe she'd put in some pickles, too. She got a jar of them down from one of the cabinets over the counter. There. That's what she'd enter in the fair.

J.D. would know something was up for sure if she didn't enter nothing in the fair. She always had. Last year she won the blue ribbon for the apple pie she put in. Got a dollar prize for it, too, but J.D. bought some nails with it.

She could remember when she was a youngun how they all entered something in the fair. Papa put in a melon or some corn he'd grown, and Mama took something from the garden or a bonnet she made and embroidered late at night when everybody else had gone to bed and left her by the lamp still working with that needle. Mama would always help Cindy fix some cookies or something. Her brothers had built enough bird houses and nest boxes for every feathered thing in the county, she reckoned. But Mama and Papa said it didn't really matter what they made so long as they tried. The fair brought out the best in everybody, showed that everybody had something good they could do. Taught younguns early to do their best. She could remember winning nickels and dimes, even a quarter once, when she was a youngun. Candy money Papa let her spend at Parrish's for sticks of black licorice and hard candy. She was surprised last year when she entered for dollars instead of quarters like the younguns. Whole dollars. She could remember one time when Mama won enough money to buy the material for a new dress and some hand lotion. Papa said she better spend every penny of it on herself, too. Only extra money Mama ever had for anything was fair money. She tried to figure out how many quarters Mama must've won.

She set the basket in the wagon. J.D. would take it for her when he went. He was taking a hog. In the pen right now getting them ready to go. She thought about how funny he was going to look going down the road with that hog in the wagon. She could see it in her mind. Just didn't look right. Of course that's what he was going to have to do was let it ride. If he tied it to the back with a rope, he'd be all day walking it to town. Besides that, you couldn't afford to walk a hog like that. Didn't want it to walk off a single pound.

She fixed J.D.'s dinner early so he could eat before he left to go to town. She hadn't fixed as much the last couple of days. J.D. had been going to the warehouse, and he'd let Baxter off till after the fair when it was time to bring in the corn. She wondered what Baxter would do after J.D. didn't need him anymore. She thought about J.D. there in the house by himself, less work to do outside, making sandwiches or opening jars of stuff she'd put up. No family, no hand, no nothing.

She closed her eyes and leaned against the counter, dizzy. She could see dresses and bonnets running, running, running across a field of daisies and not looking back. She was way too dizzy.

And she stayed kind of dizzy like that, just not as bad, for two solid days till she and J.D. got the baby and a picnic lunch in the wagon and went to the fair. All the while the women were running, night and day, asleep and awake, they were running, not looking back.

Oh, the fair. She loved it, loved everything about it. The smells of the food, hot cornbread frying.

The sounds of the animals and the way their pens smelled like dust or manure all the time. The scent of the fresh sawdust around where they had the contests. All the people talking. Younguns squealing to ride a pony even though they had one at home.

And she loved this time of the year. Seemed like she just took things for granted other times, but not now. Now it was special. The air was different this time of year. She could feel it, feel that the cold would come soon, feel that the leaves would die and fall off. But it made her tingle inside somehow, made her want to drink in every bit of life and green and warmth she could. Get it while the getting was good.

She looked at J.D. as they walked, him taking long steps, her taking shorter, faster ones trying to keep up, heading for the livestock area before the judging started. She might've known he'd have to go there first. Still, she looked at the side of his face and saw the easiness of it, the not-knowing. All he was worried about was whether that hog would place in the fair. He was sure it would.

When they finally stopped there where the hogs were, she shifted Callie from one arm to the other. Seemed like to her that baby had got heavy as a bushel of potatoes.

"You gonna be here long?" she asked J.D.

"Shh. Judging's 'bout to start."

"I'm going to find Mama."

He leaned sideways and pushed up on his toes to see around to where the judges were, not looking at her at all.

"Over there with the baked goods and preserves. J.D., you hear me?"

"Yeah," he said.

As she walked away she could hear the head judge hollering out something about the way the judging would be run. J.D would stand right there at the livestock all day long if she knew him. Wouldn't move at all except for when they broke for dinner and he went to the wagon to eat. More to see at the fair than one thing, she thought. More than one thing to see and things still to sort out in her mind even though she hadn't been able to think about another thing besides Sam and the women running through the fields for days on end. She felt like her feet weren't connected to her, like they were carrying her around but weren't really her feet at all. Had a mind of their own. Did what they wanted to do, went where they wanted to go, not where she told them to. She walked by that man playing music who had that little monkey with him, Callie reaching out toward the monkey, and past that gypsy wagon where the sign said the woman could look in her glass ball and see your future. She wanted to stop there, go right in and find out just what the old woman could see, but her feet kept right on going. She went by the place where you could have your picture made. She didn't feel much like having her picture made. Didn't have no money for it even if she'd wanted to. She felt as if that's what the 'cosin would be like for her one day, like just another picture somebody'd made, like she never lived there at all and was just looking at a picture of a house with a garden and a barn. Could be anybody's house. Just a picture.

Just a picture like any other picture except J.D. was in it, in it all by himself even though he was supposed to have a wife and youngun. Heaven have mercy on her. How had it come to this?

Her feet took her to a bench underneath a shade tree, and she sat down. She needed to rest a minute, set heavy Callie down on her lap a minute. She watched the people go by, some young, some old, some she knew, some she didn't, that had come in from all over the county, she reckoned. And she watched the wives with their husbands. You could look at them and tell which ones got along good and which ones were just fair. Not hard to tell at all when you saw them walking. Some would walk close together, say something to each other once in a while, and some would walk farther apart like her and J.D. Not hard to tell at all. Still, they were together, even if they did walk far apart. They hadn't run off from each other. Probably hadn't never even crossed their minds.

She closed her eyes and listened to the leaves over her head rustle against each other when the breeze blew. They sounded like water running far away, like the creek after a big rain.

The fair hadn't never been like this. It had always filled her head up with all that was there, always been the closest thing to really going anywhere. But now all the things at the fair just danced around the thing that was filling up her head, a real chance at going somewhere. She could see the women running, running right on past the long tables of cakes and pies, right on past the pony ride toward another field of daisies. Running, running, not looking back. Daisies far as you could see.

She opened her eyes when somebody sat down on the other end of the bench. A woman not much older than Cindy smiled at her and Callie.

"Good day," the woman said.

"Good day," Cindy said.

The woman's husband tipped his hat to her. A little boy pulled at his arm begging, "Papa, let's go over there. Over there, Papa. Over there."

She got up on her feet and went on, wondering where in the world Sam's booth might be. Her feet took her on toward wherever it was she was headed.

And finally she saw him, his booth set up there between women from a church trying to raffle off a quilt and a chimney sweep trying to drum up business before time for folks to start burning their fireplaces. Sam had all sorts of shoes, at least a dozen different kinds, out on the table in front of him. She reckoned he'd just have to pack them up in a hurry, get them together and in his car fast. He was turned sideways to her, hadn't seen her, because he was talking to a woman looking at a pair of Sunday lace-ups, smiling at her a lot like she was the best customer he ever had. Looked to be middle-age or better. Probably a widow-woman he'd sold to before.

He put the shoes in a sack, and the woman walked away. He looked her way now, but he didn't move, just stared at her, didn't call to her or nothing. Didn't want to make a scene, she supposed. Didn't even smile at her, just stared and stared, watched her close as she walked slow, toting Callie. She reckoned he wondered what she was going to do.

Didn't matter what she had to say to him nohow. Her feet would not stop, would not even slow down. Her feet went on and on toward Mama and safety, safety from doing what they knew was wrong, what she just couldn't do, no matter how bad she hated that 'cosin.

She could feel him watching her as she went on by. Still he didn't call to her. She wondered what he was thinking about her. Did he think she'd gone by and was coming back, or did he think she'd gone on by for good? Wasn't no way she could tell. Couldn't read him like she could J.D. Been reading J.D. a good while.

Her feet went on till she got to her folks, and her feet stayed with them all the rest of that day. Didn't even go back by the shoe booth at all. Stayed right there with her folks' feet till she and J.D. got in the wagon and went home.

She felt like she hadn't breathed a single time all that whole afternoon, like she was scared to breathe in deep or she'd take out running hard as she could go for that '29 Ford. It was her feet that was keeping her there, them and her breathing as little as she could, never once deep, and she knew it. How had she let it get this far?

J.D's feathers were ruffled because she'd stayed with Mama and Papa all day long and hadn't even come there to see how his hog had done. But then he hadn't bothered about seeing how she'd placed either till it was time to hand out prize money. And what if she had left Mama and Papa? It wouldn't have been J.D. she went to. Little did he know he'd better be thankful to the good Lord that she'd stayed with them all day. Little did he know it was the steadiness in their feet that kept her from running off. Never would know neither. She sure wasn't going to tell him. She'd just have to do without the clothes in that case she'd packed for Sam to pick up.

As they rode along in the wagon, she closed her eyes and held tight to Callie. She could see the women walking slow back toward the 'cosin toting daisies in their hands. How had she ever let it go so far, her thinking she could just up and leave and never come back here again?

10

○ The Women ○

Cindy stood on the front porch, leaning up against one of the columns beside the steps. It was too hot in the house, so hot she was about to faint. She breathed in the cool air fall had brought in.

Below, she could see the brown clumps where her flowers used to be. They were dead. Been dead since a couple of days after she'd gone to the fair even though they had plenty of water and sun.

Sometimes she felt that way. Dead. Like her body was moving and doing all the things she was supposed to do, only she wasn't really in it no more. The baby was what was inside. The baby and nothing else.

She looked off to the woods there at the edge of the 'cosin. Maybe she'd finally learned. That next day after the fair when J.D. had gone to pick up his hog, she had walked down there to where she left her case. It was still there. Sam hadn't picked it up at all. But he'd been there, all right. She'd toted it back up there to the house and opened it. Her clothes were all tumbled around and wrinkled. He'd come there and gone through it and left it setting right there in the woods.

Didn't matter nohow. She hadn't been able to leave then, and she couldn't leave now. Never would leave and she knew it. One baby in there in the house sleeping and another one on the way. She'd never leave here, but they would. She'd see to it.

Funny how mamas were like that. Whatever it was they wanted to do and couldn't, didn't, they'd set their minds to their younguns doing. Sell their souls for their younguns'.

Maybe that's what all the women of the 'cosin had done. Died trying to give their younguns life.

She looked across the road at the weeds over there that were turning brown. Brown like the drying corn Baxter and J.D. were picking right now. She wondered how he was going to take it when she told him about the baby. Another mouth to feed. Another time of hoping he'd get a boy to carry on with the farm.

Didn't matter to her if it was a boy or not. Still wasn't gonna spend his life in this 'cosin. Wasn't gonna have to stand here on this porch looking off down the road wanting to see more than just trees and not being able to see a thing.

She looked at the shape of the road that seemed to come into the 'cosin from both ways, but not to lead out. Like the half moon. Half Moon 'Cosin. You could reach for the moon, and you'd either get it or not get it. Half didn't mean a thing.

In the kitchen she stoked the fire in the stove, and sat down in a chair while she waited for it to get good and hot. She looked at the jars of beets and string beans she'd set out for dinner. Looked nice all preserved in jars and sealed tight, but cut off from their own roots. Not really alive at all anymore.

She looked at the frying pan Mama gave her hanging against the wall on a hook. Mama had always been happy in her kitchen, not like Cindy at all. And Mama gave her that pan and thought she'd learn to be happy in a kitchen of her own.

That was the difference between her and Mama, she reckoned.

Mama knew how to take things like they were and never ask what they might have been. Cindy never had learned to do that. Always wondering. Always asking. Maybe if you never asked you never found out you weren't happy with the way things were.

After a while she got up and made her biscuits, singing a slow, sad song as she rolled them between her hands. A ballad. That's how ballads came to be, she reckoned, people singing about folks like her, folks that reached for the moon and got half of it.

She put the biscuits in the oven and heated the string beans in a pot. Looked alive, sure enough, but they weren't. Just hulls preserved.

She brought Callie from the bedroom and set her on the kitchen floor while she put dinner on the table. She watched the baby crawl up under the table like she was hiding. Funny the way little younguns thought. She'd bet Callie thought that just because she couldn't see Cindy's face, couldn't see nothing but her feet, that Cindy couldn't see her either. But she could see the baby plain as day up under that table. Funny the way little younguns thought. Thought things would always be the same, like they'd never grow up and live out on their own, like somebody'd always be there to keep them from harm. Thought they were the center of the world and everything always turns out for the best.

She pulled Callie out from under the table and fed her her dinner. Babies were special things, very special things. They were the thing that gave you a reason to go on, gave you a little hope because you kept telling yourself things would be different for them. But they were the thing, sometimes, that kept it from being any different.

J.D. and Baxter talked at dinner about how much corn they had left to pick, how winter was coming on. They'd finish next week just in time for Thanksgiving. Maybe that's when she'd tell J.D. her news, after he finished bringing in the crop and had time to sit down and rest awhile.

Sometimes she wished she'd have a slow time where she could rest. She wondered if J.D. ever thought about that, that he got a little time off in the dead of winter, had less work to do. She never had less work to do. Always had a house to keep, meals to cook. Come summer she was in the garden. Come winter she was catching up on whatever it was she'd let go when everything in the garden was coming off and she was putting it up. Sometimes she wondered where it would all end.

It all ended where she ended, she reckoned. Ended back there by the creek where all the women that came here before her were buried.

J.D. talked about what he'd do when it was good and cold, how he'd kill hogs and cure the hams. How he'd grind sausage and put it in the casings. How he'd chop and split wood that would last them through the winter and on till the next year when he'd do it again. He talked and talked, on and on till he and Baxter went back to the field. J.D. loved the winter.

She never had liked winter one bit, never had liked how it was brown and gray, everything dried up and dead. But like it or not, winter was coming on.

After dinner she picked up the pecans that had fallen from the tree out near the smokehouse. She'd put most of them in the pantry to keep, but she'd crack enough of them next week to have pecan pie at Thanksgiving.

She thought about Mama's pecan pies. She made the best pies in the world. She couldn't count the hours Mama spent in the kitchen rolling out crusts, breaking up the pecans into small pieces. And Mama never seemed to mind all those hours a bit. Funny how she wasn't like Mama in that way at all.

She could remember Mama saying so when she was a youngun. She'd sneak out and go down there to the barn where Papa was sawing lumber and sniff and sniff the scent of the sawdust till the inside of her nose burned and she was dizzy. She always loved that smell. And she always loved to watch Papa build something. She could remember a few times when Papa let her have his hammer and some nails. She played with the scrap ends of boards he cut off. Sometimes she would nail them to the trees, and he'd get mad. Papa always swore up and down she was gonna kill every tree in their yard. But every one of them trees was still living to this day except the pine lightning had hit. Mama always said

Cindy would grow out of it, learn to be like her, learn what a joy it was to run a house and raise a family. And Mama thought what she was saying was right, but it wasn't. It just wasn't. But then Mama never dreamed big and she never lived in this 'cosin, either.

Cindy set a full bucket of pecans off to the side and started again with the empty one. She listened to how the pecans hit the bottom of the empty bucket, the sound echoing off the sides of the bucket like your voice would echo off the trees at night when everything was still and quiet.

Seemed like the blood was rushing to her head, and all she could hear was the pecans echoing and the creek water, running. She felt dizzy, way too dizzy, like she was up in the top of the pecan tree instead of here on the ground. She looked down from the top of the tree and saw four high necked dresses, four bonnets to hold the hair, picking up pecans beneath the tree in Half Moon 'Cosin.